# THE MIN-MIN

Mavis Thorpe Clark

# THE MIN-MIN

THE MACMILLAN COMPANY

Gulla Tank is an imaginary out-station and
all characters in the book are fictional.

The Macmillan Company
Collier-Macmillan Canada, Ltd., Toronto, Ontario

Library of Congress catalog card number: 79-78086

*Printed in the United States of America*

FIRST PRINTING

# ♔ Glossary

*Aborigine*—an Australian native, descended from the earliest inhabitants of the continent.

*billy-can*—a tin can with a lid and a wire handle over the top, used mainly to boil water over a fire.

*billy-cart*—a wheeled cart, generally made from a wooden soapbox and guided with a pair of rope reins.

*black-tracker*—an Aborigine skilled at following the tracks of a fugitive, man or beast.

*bore*—a well, with a windmill-powered pump to bring the water to the surface.

*bull dust*—the fine dust, inches thick, that lies on any main outback road in the summer.

*chalk-ee*—a schoolteacher.

*corroboree*—a ceremonial gathering of Aborigines, with singing, dancing and acting.

*crutching*—removing the dirty portions of a sheep's fleece.

*dead-finish*—the local name for a large woody bush with sharp spikes.

*dilly bag*—a string bag made out of plant or animal fibers.

*dingo*—the Australian native dog, that often attacks sheep.

*dog fence*—a wire-netting fence, four-and-a-half feet high, erected by the government across South Australia to keep the dingoes out of the sheep country.

*dogger*—a man employed to trap and kill dingoes.

*fettler*—a man employed on the railway line to keep the tracks in good condition.

*fly-wire*—wire screening.

*free-lite*—a wind-driven propeller that generates electricity.

*galah*—a beautiful Australian parrot, but a derogatory term when used to describe a person.

*ganger*—the foreman in charge of a group of fettlers.

*gibbers*—the small stones found lying over thousands of miles of the dry inland area of Australia.

*jackeroo*—a young man who is learning all aspects of running a sheep-station.

*joey*—a young kangaroo.

*mate*—friend.

*mill*—a windmill at a bore.

*Min-Min*—the Aboriginal name for a light, low in the sky, that is sometimes seen in the desert country.

*motor-bike cowboy*—a stockman who rounds up livestock on a motorcycle instead of on a horse.

*mulga*—a stunted tree with needle-like foliage.

*muster*—a round-up of livestock.

*narked*—annoyed.

*nulla nulla*—an Aboriginal weapon, like a club.

*off-sider*—cook's helper.

*outback*—the isolated inland areas of Australia.

*out-station*—a hut or house for a stockman some miles from the main homestead on a station.

*quandong stone*—the stone of the wild peach.

*sheep-station*—a ranch where sheep are raised.

*sleepers*—the heavy wooden cross-bars that support the rails of a railway track.

*smoke-oh*—the morning or afternoon work break.

*swag*—the rolled blanket carried by a tramp.

*swagman; swaggie*—a tramp.

*sweets* or *lollies*—candy.

*tailing*—removing the tails of the young lambs.

*tucker-box*—a lunch box or basket.

*wagon*—a railroad freight car.

*water bag*—a canteen.

*willy-willy*—a vertical spiral of red dust.

*woomera*—an Aboriginal throwing stick.

*wurlie*—an Aboriginal hut built of boughs and leaves.

# THE MIN-MIN

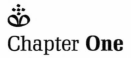

# Chapter **One**

SYLVIE PICKED UP the shopping basket from the kitchen table. The weekly "Tea and Sugar," a slow mixed goods train which ran on the rails that spanned the southern desert of the Australian continent, was almost due.

The top edging of the cane basket was broken, and the ends sharp. Sylvie had to be careful to carry the barbed points away from her bare legs. The piece of paper with the list of extra provisions to buy from the train was lying on the bottom. The main grocery order always had to be placed a week in advance, and was brought by the "Tea and Sugar" from Port Augusta.

Her mother had put the piece of paper there an hour ago, and handed the purse to her.

"Look after it," she warned. "Don't put it down, and don't lose it."

Then she had gone into the bedroom across the narrow passage and closed the door. Sylvie knew that she would lie down on the bed in her clothes and go to sleep. She generally woke later, undressed, and got into bed properly. She had gone to sleep very quickly tonight—even before she had had time to drink the cup of tea that Sylvie made for her.

It was like this every Saturday night. There was a party each Saturday afternoon at Quinn's place—one of the single row of fettlers' homes that comprised this railway siding. From here, during the week, the men worked up and down the line, maintaining the rails of the east-west railway. But on Saturdays most of the grownups from the ten cottages gathered at Quinn's to listen to the football broadcast from as far away as Melbourne, in Victoria, or the races, and to drink beer. At evening, her mother came home and gave her and the other four children their tea—or rather supervised Sylvie giving the other four their tea—and then went to bed. Sometimes Sylvie thought her mother didn't enjoy these gatherings very much. But she understood how cut off she would be if she didn't go. Her father usually came home very late; sometimes she didn't hear him come, though most times he was noisy. He was in an ugly mood if he was quiet.

The "Tea and Sugar" didn't always come in this late on a Saturday evening, but Sylvie was glad when it did. It was one of the adult tasks that gave her satisfaction. There were so many other things she had to do that were just work.

With the basket over her arm, she turned into the passage. She passed the closed door without a glance, but she looked in at the second. Two of the other four, Billie and Reg, slept here. Billie was the baby—he was nearly four—and Reg was eleven. In due course there would be another baby. That was why her mother tired quickly. There would be more work to do then, less room in the cottage, and the money for food would have to stretch to include the newcomer. Sylvie wasn't looking forward to the new baby. She hoped it wouldn't cry too much. It would be one more for her father to shout at when the mood took him. Babies, she thought, too, should be born into homes where there was always plenty of milk and butter to spread thickly.

She noticed now that Billie was uncovered, and crossed the room to his bed. These November days the temperature often rose above 100°, but the nights could have a cold tang. Billie was keeping his nose warm by burying it in the pillow, while his tail was the pinnacle of a bare arch. She pushed him down gently, his body warm to her touch. She rolled him over on his side and covered him up. He was heavy with sleep. Reg was asleep, too; she could see only the top of his dark head—the rest of him was under the bedclothes. She remembered that he used to sleep with his tail up like Billie.

She paused for a moment at the side of Reg's bed. She wished that he hadn't done the things he had done today. There would be trouble, and he would be punished. Perhaps even taken away, as the policeman from Kingoonya had threatened last time, when it was proved that he was the one who had put the detonators on the line, and caused the express train, the Trans, to be delayed for twenty minutes.

She only glanced through the open doorway of the room she shared with Ann and Ruby. She knew that Ann would be clutching a hairless teddy bear. She thought the kid, at seven, ought to be old enough to go to bed without that thing. Well, when the rest of the stuffing fell out, there would be no more teddy. The imitation fur skin would not stand any more stitches. She looked at Ruby's bed long enough to note the humped-up blankets on the iron bedstead. Ruby was nine. She could look after herself. And Sylvie was glad she was too much of a sleepy-head to stay awake late enough to go with her to the "Tea and Sugar." She liked to go alone.

She stepped onto the veranda that ran the width of the house, the fly-wire door squeaking on its hinges behind her. There was no moon yet, and the stars were white and high. The earth was dark except for a few separated lights down on the line. It was a smooth darkness, broken only by the darker shapes of the ten square houses. There were no trees or bushes on the slopes of this shallow basin to add extra shadows. From each house a narrow oblong of light escaped through the fly-wire doors, none of which fitted snugly, due to constant banging.

At the side of the cottage steps she paused to put the basket into the old wheelbarrow before pushing it ahead of her down the slope. She would need the barrow to carry the main order of groceries.

Then she heard the grumbling rhythm of the approaching train. It was still a mile or so away, and distance and night made it sound like wind in the earth's stomach. The sound swelled and grew louder, and suddenly she saw the train snaking down from the plain into this depression.

As there was only one passenger carriage, the train was not well lit—just a lamp here and there on a long line of wagons. The engine siren gave a long impatient blast as the train lessened speed. It wanted all the siding people down at the track quickly with their baskets and money. It was not stabling here for the night but moving farther along the line.

Other people began to come from the houses, carrying baskets, pushing wheelbarrows, prams, or billy-carts.

Sylvie didn't notice the cold stones under her bare feet as she pushed the barrow down the slope. She was the oldest girl at the siding but she seldom wore shoes. The few pairs she had ever possessed had, in turn, been worn out by the other four children.

Some of the people hurrying with her were women who had been at the party at Quinn's. They were laughing and noisy, but she didn't talk to them. It would spoil her special, secret enjoyment.

A small group soon collected. She scanned them quickly, relieved to see that her father was not among them. By the time the line of wagons pulled up, metal grating on metal, there were about twenty people clustered in the darkness beside the track. There was no platform, just a water tank and a shelter hut for the man on duty when the trains went through. Most of them did not stop, only a few of the goods with freight to pick up or put down.

Sylvie edged to the front of the crowd, leaving her barrow in an accessible spot. She wanted to be first in when they opened the door of the provision van. Light spilled like liquid then onto the stones, and turned the weathered bits of broken bottle into diamonds. But it was the inside of the van she liked. It was fitted like a shop. There was color and light and orderliness . . . and much to look at.

She was about to spring onto the van steps when she saw Clive Scott jump from the passenger carriage. The schoolteacher! Fear jabbed her. He wasn't expected back until Sunday night. He had left last night on a fast goods to go down to Port Augusta and then by bus to Whyalla. She knew he visited a girl named Myrtle, who was a trainee nurse in the hospital there. Something must have happened to change his plans. Perhaps Myrtle had had to work an extra shift. That had happened before. But Sylvie wished it hadn't happened this weekend.

Now the things that had been done to the schoolroom would be discovered before their father had time to go off to work up the line on Monday. That would make things worse for Reg, who had been the ringleader in the destruction.

The crowd greeted the young schoolteacher with varying degrees of heartiness, but with no mention of the destruction in the schoolroom. Anyone would think they didn't know about it.

"Hello there!" Clive Scott smiled cheerily at her. "Your turn to do the shopping?"

"Yes." She turned away quickly, lest he see her guilty look. Clive Scott wasn't very old—not quite twenty, someone had found out—but he looked at you so straight that, even if you weren't guilty yourself, you felt guilty for the others, like Reg and the Timms boys.

She hopped up into the van, trying not to let the teacher's return disturb the pleasure that she had been anticipating all day. She was followed quickly by the other shoppers.

The reds and yellows and greens of the fresh fruits and vegetables were as gaudy as the packets of sweets, biscuits, cigarettes, and some tinned foods on the opposite shelves, all brilliant in contrast to the outside blackness. The men and women who came out of the blackness were made instantly a little light-headed. They leaned on the counter, exchanging jokes and gossip with the attendant. They were noisy, some of them not very clean, and if any of them were young, the youth was hidden under the lines of hard living.

Although Sylvie was first into the van, she didn't hasten to ask for her box of ordered groceries. She liked time to look at the well-stocked shelves and the rainbow hues of the labels on the tinned food, especially the seafoods. There were sea pictures on these labels and drawings of graceful fish. They were very gay. She pretended that fish was on her list tonight, so that the attendant would pass her a couple of tins for inspection. But tinned fish was never on the list. It was too expensive for a large family; and so she had to shake her head and pass them back. And then there were the jams. These labels were very beautiful, too. Pictures of fruit on these. Fat scarlet strawberries, round-bellied black currants like aniseed balls. She had never seen these growing, had never seen many fruit trees at all. But jam was always part of the main order, and was never strawberry or black currant. It was generally plum, which was so much cheaper—or melon, which was cheaper again.

Her eyes roamed from shelf to shelf wishing she might, just once, buy one of the fancy packets of cheese. But her list—which itemized only bread, milk, fruit, vegetables, and meat—was inflexible. Mum had made that clear from the time she had brought home two packets of chocolate biscuits.

So she put the bread and the cartons of milk into her basket and, with a sigh, turned to the fruit and vegetables. The polish on the apples brightened her again, and she knew enough about pea pods to see that they were fresh.

Then the attendant pushed the previously ordered box of groceries under her nose. This was his way of reminding her that there was still the meat to buy in the refrigerated van next door, and the "Tea and Sugar" was in a hurry to reach its stable.

She carried the box of groceries out to the wheelbarrow first, her arms straining around the weight. Then she returned for the basket, which she also emptied into the barrow. With the empty basket on her arm, she passed on to the butcher's van. Since the railways supplied a kerosene refrigerator to each house, her list of meat was enough to last a week. But the meat van held no interest for her and—though she always pretended to the butcher that she knew quality—she made her purchases quickly.

Her basket was heavy again. She rested it on the edge of the landing while she jumped from the top step. People were still talking in the shadows beyond reach of the light. They didn't like the light, as she did. Before dragging the basket from its high perch, she felt in her pocket to make sure the purse was still there. She would have to account for the money and the change in the morning, when her mother woke up.

As she turned away, the van door was shut behind her, gathering in the light. Slowly at first the wheels began to roll, the rhythmic grumbling grew louder and louder as the "Tea and Sugar" climbed the gentle grade.

The wheel of Sylvie's barrow was rusty. It grated on the stones and was heavy to push. She began to make her way around the people. Clive Scott was still with them, talking to Mrs. Hedges with whom he boarded. Mrs. Hedges was the ganger's wife; she was the only woman at the siding who didn't have any children. That was why she had a spare room for the schoolteacher. She was a little round woman, who put on a clean fancy-worked apron every day. Each fortnight she went down to the Port to have her hair set. Sylvie thought it always looked beautiful.

"Hello there." The teacher was speaking to her again. "That barrow's too heavy for you—I'll push it."

"No-o . . . " She was remembering the schoolroom—the dreadful mess of it—the broken record player. "No-o."

"Give it to me. It'll break your back."

She passed it over silently. She really wanted him to push it. It was the kind of thing he would do for Myrtle, the girl he liked. She had seen Myrtle once: a thin girl—thin as she was herself—with fair hair with the shine of the sun in it, only she pulled it back too tightly and some of the shine was lost.

She felt important walking up the hill beside him. She wished she had shoes on. He had told her once that he thought she ought to wear shoes, that later on, when she was older, it would be hard to fit her feet into the strange narrow shoes women wore. She wished she could think of something to say, something that was sensible and adult. He would expect that of her—she was his oldest pupil, much too old, actually, for the sixth grade which was his highest age group.

But this was a distinction that did not trouble her, and she thought now, with great satisfaction, that Mr. Scott would be teaching her next year too! Her father seldom listened to pleas but he had conceded—as she seemed to be making most unusual headway with this teacher—that she could have the benefit of his two-year term. After that, of course, she would have to get a job in one of the shops at the Port, or else at one of the larger sheep stations where the cook sometimes had a young off-sider. She had been told, often enough, that a woman who could cook for a team was always sure of a job. Well, she didn't have to think about that until the end of next year.

Just as they neared the top of the slope, with the ten square shapes of the cottages before them, the few lights of the siding still pale below them, and some people still talking, Sylvie looked sideways across the stretch of plain . . . and there was the dancing light.

"A min-min!" she cried.

Quickly, Clive Scott let the barrow rest on the stony ground.

"Where? I've never seen one—in the whole nine months I've been here. I was beginning to think it was a fairy tale you told me, Sylvie."

"There it is!"

They looked across the gibber plain, flat as a board to the horizon, where a slight shading in the depth of darkness indicated where earth and sky became one. There were no stars low in the sky—at least no ordinary stars. But there was a small light, suspended just above the earth shadow. It gleamed white with diamond points, and then the color merged to pink. With the change, it swayed from side to side as though on an invisible thread from heaven. Then it moved toward them.

"Someone's walking out there, carrying a hurricane lamp," Clive said, without conviction.

"No!" The girl was excited. "I've seen it before. I've walked toward it."

"In the night?"

"You only see it in the night."

"And what happened?"

"As I walked toward it, it started to go farther away—I couldn't catch up with it. But when I turned, it followed me."

"Were you frightened?"

"No. But it's queer, isn't it?"

"P'raps it's a car."

She was scornful. "You know there aren't any tracks over there."

"A kangaroo shooter, maybe."

"No, the shooters don't go that way."

Clive Scott laughed. "All right, Sylvie—you win. I know a light like this has been reported from many scattered lonely parts of the continent—under different names of course. Some call it a Jack o' Lantern."

"What do you really think it is, Mr. Scott?"

"Oh-h, a natural phenomenon of some sort. In Queensland oil men say it's the underground fumes escaping to the surface and igniting."

"That's not the same as a min-min!" Sylvie said firmly. "Old Jack, the Aborigine, told me about it. He said it beckons people—but it never lets them catch up. It makes me feel excited inside—as though I'll just have to run after it and try to catch it." Her voice was bubbly. "After I take the shopping in, Mr. Scott, would you go with me—and we'll try?" She was eager.

The schoolteacher laughed. "Not at this hour of the night, Sylvie. In any case, it's a long way to the horizon."

"Look, it's turned bright pink!"

They watched the strange star glow like a pale ruby and swing provocatively, like a hip dancer, toward them. Then it began to dim.

"It's going . . . " Sylvie said, her voice flat. They watched as the light faded into blackness. "Some night," said the girl, "I'm going to keep walking until I come to it."

The schoolteacher took up the handles of the barrow and they started off again. "But you just told me the Aborigines say you can't catch up with it."

"Well, I could prove that, couldn't I?"

"M'mm . . . Well, here we are. Can you manage to carry these things into the house?"

"Yes. Thank you for pushing the barrow." Her excitement had died, and she was worrying again. "You . . . you're not going to the schoolroom tonight?"

"No, indeed. I'm going to bed."

"Goodnight." She thought her voice sounded too relieved. She hoped it wouldn't make him suspicious, make him go to the schoolroom.

"Goodnight."

She stood by the barrow and watched him turn in the direction of Hedges' cottage. That satisfied her—the schoolroom was the opposite way. Then she took up the first basketful of provisions and went up the steps, kicking open the wire door with her bare foot and going into the warm darkness of the passage. The house was quiet. Her father must still be at Quinn's. She went unerringly into the kitchen. When the first load was safely on the table, she switched on the light.

It was a poor light. There had been no wind for days—an unusual calm—and the propeller on the tall tower of the wind-driven free-lite had not turned enough to charge the row of batteries on the back veranda. If the wind didn't get up soon, they would have to get out the kerosene lamps. She knew she should use the lamp now and not drain the batteries, but she hated lighting the kerosene lamp, having seen one blow up once.

She brought the rest of the goods from the barrow. Even in the dull light, the colors on the labels seemed to glow. She opened the cupboard door. No order here like the provision van. The first few things she put on the shelves looked so utterly different in these surroundings that she took them out and began again. First of all, she removed everything from the shelves: dishes, cooking utensils, empty jars, all elbowing the jam and the tea and the sugar. She would make it all as neat and shining as the van and tomorrow, perhaps, her mother would not have such a bad headache.

There were so many things on the shelves, things that were never used, like the old grater and the rusty egg whisk. She would like to have taken those out to the rubbish heap, but she knew she dare not. Soon all the floor around her, right to the door, held piles of articles sorted into their separate groups. It would be so much easier for Mum to find everything when they were all put back in groups on the shelves.

She became absorbed, and didn't notice time. Now and again she came across an article she hadn't seen before, or had forgotten, like the butter dish with the picture of the Sydney Harbor Bridge on it. Sometimes her mother talked about Sydney. That was where she had been born, she had told Sylvie once. And once Sylvie had heard her mum beg her father to go back there. She still felt frightened when she remembered the row they had had. Her father had said that he could never go back, that there was no place for him anywhere but in this out-of-the-way desert spot.

Sylvie knew that her father had done something, a long time ago. Something that was wrong, she was sure. But memory didn't take her back that far, and no one had ever told her what it was. She only remembered this siding, or similar sidings, and the cottages, and the steel rails which, if you stood and looked at them, became a single rail in the long distance.

She wiped the shelves before she started to put things back. It was a slow task, arranging the new packets and tins so that the labels showed to advantage, grouping the plates and the cups and the saucers so that they weren't crowding the tea and the flour and the cereal. The light became dimmer as she worked, but she didn't notice that either.

Then she heard the front door kick open and bang shut, her father's heavy, uncertain tread. Surely he was earlier than usual! She noticed with panic that he wasn't singing, that he was quiet. She stared at the doorway, waiting for him to appear. Even then she didn't notice that the pile of saucepans had been pushed so far over that they were just inside the doorway.

He stood in the opening for a second. He was a man of middle height, with a whipcord sparseness about him, and his head and shoulders thrust a little forward because he bent slightly at the waistline. Deep furrows ran from nose to chin in either cheek, and his eyes were as blue as the background label on a fish tin. Not that he always opened his eyes wide enough for the blue to be seen; they were generally half closed like the eyes of many men who work continuously in strong sunlight. His hands were strong, sunpocked, and calloused.

He peered at her. "Cripes! what a mess. And this light —what yer got this light on for—at this hour!" He took a step toward the switch and his foot landed in the pile of pots. Down he went, falling heavily. There was a bump as he struck his head on the leg of the table. Sylvie sprang up and ran to him.

"Dad!" she cried fearfully.

He sat up, rubbing his head. "What d'ye think you're doing!" he blazed at her.

"I was tidying the shelves . . . for Mum . . . making them look pretty."

"Pretty! Shelves look pretty! What rubbish are you talking! Get this junk away—damn quick!"

Hastily Sylvie dragged the pots to her, throwing them into the cupboard, higgledy-piggledy, disturbing the nice arrangement of her tins. What did it matter—the nice arrangement? More than likely Mum's headache wouldn't let her notice anyway.

"Hurry up—get this junk away! I want to get this light off!"

Sylvie worked as fast as she could, scrambling under the table to reach things rather than pass her father who still sat on the floor, rubbing his head and glowering through his thick eyelashes. When the last tin, the last cup, and the last packet were back on the cupboard shelf, she slammed the door shut and shot past him. Even so she caught the stinging swing of his open palm on her bare leg.

"That's right—get yer monkey-face out of it!" he snarled.

Just for a second, the girl stood in the doorway, her hand

to her leg. "I'm too big to hit," her voice trembled with tears and anger and disappointment. "Mum says I'm too big to hit!"

"You'll never be too big as long as you're in my house, girl—never too big."

Sylvie didn't wait for him to get to his feet. She sped along the passage and into the bedroom she shared with Ruby and Ann. She didn't put on the light. Quickly she dragged off the shrunken sweater and the too-short dress, even though the hem had been let down to the limit, dropping them and her underclothing on the end of the bed. From under her pillow, she drew a rumpled nightgown, and then burrowed, like Reg, down under the blankets.

"I won't stay! I won't stay!" she said aloud, and Ruby muttered sleepily and said, "What yer say, Sylvie?"

Sylvie cried into the pillow, "I won't stay! I won't stay!"

Ruby muttered again, but she didn't wake up, and Ann turned onto her other side and said two indistinct words, which Sylvie knew to be "Where's teddy?" Still crying, she got up, felt around under Ann's warm bedclothes, and put the stuffed animal back into Ann's arms.

## Chapter **Two**

SYLVIE DID NOT sleep well that night. Not that she cried for long. She stopped crying because tears prevented her thinking, and she had a lot of thinking to do. Not about her father or the blow he had given her, but about the school. There would be trouble about that, which would bring her father back into the picture in a different way. And Reg, something would happen to Reg over this. She felt frightened for him, and for herself.

With the first light she rose and put on her clothes. She dressed quietly. Neither Ruby nor Ann was awake though they had had many more hours of sleep than she. Ruby looked like a beautiful doll with her gold curls lying over the pillow, and her pink mouth. Sylvie admired her sister's beauty; it gave her a satisfied feeling inside. She looked at Ann. The little girl still had the teddy bear close to her, though she was not clutching it so tightly. Ann was quite different from Ruby. She was like Sylvie, herself. Straight hair without much color and a thin small face. Her eyes were the same color as Sylvie's—a hazel that was sometimes green, sometimes brown. Not the dark velvet-brown eyes of Ruby.

Sylvie closed the bedroom door as she went out, hoping Ruby hadn't been pretending sleep, to follow her. She wanted to manage this piece of trouble on her own.

As she stepped off the veranda, the black-edged ball of sun came over the horizon. Already the eastern sky was

glowing red, shot here and there with the indigo blue of a
mocking streak of cloud. In this direction nothing ob-
structed her view of the sun's movement. Not a tree was
between her and the horizon. The small, dark brown gibbers
that covered the country glowed as the sun poured over
them. The earth looked as though countless loads of brown
metal had been tipped and spread evenly over it. There was
not a touch of green anywhere; the last of the hardy succu-
lent plants had long since perished for lack of rain.

The sun and sky were dominant, infinitely vaster and
greater than earth. Sylvie stood to watch the glowing spec-
tacle as the sun moved quickly above the horizon. It was
surely climbing at the very spot where the min-min had
danced last night! For the moment even the schoolroom was
forgotten.

Below her the rails were black and deceitfully cold-look-
ing in the hot light. Apart from the water tank and shelter
hut, the only sign of habitation was the straight row of railway cottages behind her, and the school building. The cottages were square with roofs like square Chinese hats, and
were raised two or three feet on stilts to cheat the white ants.
Their many legs made them look like fat square centipedes.

The houses had recently been painted in pastel shades of
pink, blue, beige, and green, and the roofs silver-frosted.
But this sign of care didn't offset the litter of parts of old
cars, cardboard cartons, broken toys, bottles, on which the
first layer of red dust, blown in by the filthy wind from across
the Nullarbor Plain, had already settled.

But she was watching the sun, not looking at the litter.
She watched until the sun was well above the earth's rim
and the movement slowing down, then she turned toward the
school. It was a large weatherboard room, built like a hall

with a gabled roof, standing in a pebbled yard. The tank attached had not had any water in it for the last nine months, but once, a long time ago, when they had first come to the siding, she had seen it overflow. Up the hill a little, solitary, was the boys' outhouse, its door gaping. Guy ropes from each corner, attached to red gum posts ten feet away, kept the building anchored to the ground when the winds blew.

Her step quickened when she noticed that the schoolroom door was closed. She knew it had been left open yesterday, and ran the last few yards to try the knob. She half expected, hoped, to find it locked. But how could it be locked when they had broken the lock? It gaped immediately at her touch, and she stepped inside.

There was no change. It was just as she had seen it yesterday. The room was in chaos. Exercise books lay scattered and torn, desks upturned. The lock had been broken off Clive Scott's own cupboard, and his textbooks, boxes of chalk, pencils, and new exercise books had been trampled on. The vase with the bit of late Sturt pea—so prized by Mr. Scott and so scarce this year—lay broken and emptied on the floor, the black eyes of the flowers dead. The water had dried, leaving a stain. And there was the record player beside it, with its front bashed in. She shivered as she looked at the record player. Reg had done that.

She took the broom from the cupboard beside the door and advanced into the middle of the room, staring around at the mess. She wished she had tried to stop them. It all looked so much worse now, knowing that the teacher was back. When he had left on Friday night it had seemed that he would be away for ages.

She held the broom tightly as she stood there. She was tall for her age and thin, but taking shape, with thin arms and legs. Her cotton dress was faded, the waistline far too high, her feet bare. Her face showed that she had not had enough sleep.

The squeak of the door made her look around. She wasn't surprised to see Mr. Scott standing there. But she wished she wasn't holding the broom. It convicted her.

He didn't look at the mess, he looked straight at her. She knew then that he had been into the schoolroom last night. She had never seen him so angry before. His eyes were black.

He thrust at her. "How much of it did you do?"

"Me?" Her eyes widened. "I didn't do anything."

"Don't lie to me!"

"I ain't."

"But you knew about it?"

That made her look away.

"Your brother—young Reg—he'd be the ringleader, no doubt?"

She looked back at him. "I wouldn't know."

"Of course not." He was sarcastic. "You didn't do it—you don't know who did it! I suppose you just dreamed about a mess in the schoolroom last night—and got up at dawn to clean it up. I hate people who can't tell the truth."

He was a very young teacher, and very angry. Hands thrust hard into the pockets of his trousers, he revolved slowly on his heels, surveying the shambles. He was of medium height, square-shouldered. There was a square strength about his face, too, and his brown hair was red-tinged and wiry. Anger and the heat of the morning had already caused a wet patch to appear across the back of his shirt.

"I paid for that record player," he said; "bought it specially for this school, as an auditory aid—cost me a good many weeks' wages."

Sylvie couldn't bear to look at it then—Mr. Scott's own record player! She heard again the dreadful crunching sound as the player hit the floor—heard Reg's excited yell. Until that moment she had stood at the door watching . . . watching the mad assault on the tidiness and the learning. This kind of thing had happened before with previous teachers. She herself had taken part in other demonstrations against authority. Not for any particular reason, only because it was against authority. This time she had only looked on. She hardly knew why. But she had not remonstrated or called any of the adults to interfere. That would have set her apart from her kind. She had just watched passively— until Reg dropped the record player.

In a way, it had been an accident. Soon after the rampage started someone—it was probably Reg—had shouted, "Let's play the hurdy-gurdy!" knowing that Clive Scott never permitted any of them to handle his record player.

But to their frustration they found there were no records in the teacher's locked cupboard. Then someone remembered having seen him taking them down to Mrs. Hedges' cottage on the Friday afternoon. "Chalk-ee said he was going to make a list of the titles he had before going down to the Port—blast 'im!"

Then Reg's mate, Timmsee, had tried to start the turntable revolving, and hadn't succeeded. Reg had declared that he knew how the thing worked, pushed Timmsee aside and twisted the knobs. That started them off on a laughing, friendly scuffle. In between dodging and giving blows, each had a twist of the knobs. Then, for no reason at all, Reg picked up the player just as Timmsee poked a left at him. Falling backward, Reg dropped the machine.

As it hit the floor, Sylvie sprang into the schoolroom. "Look what you've done!" she screamed.

Reg had kicked the record player, staving in the sound grille.

"Stop it, Reg! What's Mr. Scott going to say!"

Everyone else had laughed, and Reg had laughed, too.

"You got some queer ideas about this teacher-bloke, Sylv! You seem to think he's different from the rest. But he ain't. Just a chalk-ee. Look at the way he makes us work—the homework he gives us—and the way he goes to the old man or the old woman soon as we do something he doesn't like."

"He takes us on excursions," Sylvie defended the teacher, "an' he reads books to us after school."

"He only took us on two excursions."

"That was because everyone belly-ached about them."

"Well, it was Saturday afternoon—and you don't have to go to school on Saturday."

"It wasn't school."

"Learning all about silly stones and plants *is* school. Aw-w, I'd have liked his excursions all right if they hadn't been on Saturday. But Saturday's for our own affairs—see? We couldn't let him use up our Saturdays." Reg swaggered a little. "Anyway, he only had the excursions when he first came—trying to get sweet, I reckon."

"He'd have gone on having them if you and the rest had behaved better."

"You're getting old, grown-up," Reg accused her. "S'pose you can't help it—seein' you're older than all of us."

Sylvie wondered herself if that was why she hadn't wanted to join in this lark. Last year, with any other teacher, she would have been in it.

"Anyway, you've made enough mess!" she said angrily.

Reg looked around with satisfaction. "Reckon we have; it'll show 'im, anyway."

They had all run out then, laughing, talking, giving a final kick to any book in their path. She had followed them slowly, surprised at the depression that weighted her feet.

Looking at the mess now, looking at Clive Scott's disappointed, angry face, she wished she had stopped them—tried to, anyway.

"I was told, when I was posted here, that I was coming to a very difficult school," he said to her. "That you were a lot of young toughs. All this," he pointed around him, "is just to tell me that you're proud of that reputation, eh? Afraid I might think you were softening up?"

Sylvie didn't answer. She hadn't thought of it like that. It was just something that happened—like a measles plague —every now and again. It was exciting—even the grownups found it exciting. They talked about it for a long time, enjoyed the visit from the coppers and the haranguing from the Education Department's inspector.

"Do you know," he said, "I came here because I wanted to! That's funny, isn't it?"

Sylvie stared back with those large green-brown eyes. He would have to say more if she was to know what he meant.

"I've always wanted to be a teacher—and to teach where it would do the most good. I was warned that there was no respect for education here—even by the parents. I suppose that's because some of them haven't discovered its value themselves. That's why I wanted to come. I wanted to show you what education could do for you—what it meant. But you're a hopeless lot. I can't do any good with you." His eyes clouded. "I suppose it means I'm a failure."

"No!" The denial came swiftly. "No, you're the best we've had."

"This mess doesn't suggest that! Oh, I've known I wasn't

getting through to you—try as I would—but I wasn't expecting . . . this."

Sylvie saw the depth of his disappointment. He looked so young too—a disappointed boy. But she thought it funny that he took it this way. It wasn't because of him, particularly, that they had done it. It was just something that got into the kids every now and again.

"Well, someone's going to pay for that record player!" He was savage again. "I'm not going to stand that loss— out of my own pocket!"

He couldn't explain to Sylvie that it wasn't just the money loss that was hurting so much, but that he had bought it to help them—to make his teaching alive and interesting and lasting. It was also the first expensive article he had ever owned, the first gathering of worthwhile possessions, and to see it treated so wantonly was a personal hurt.

"Looks as though Reg's prank is going to cost your father quite a bit of money."

The girl looked at him startled. This was a contingency that hadn't entered her mind.

"He didn't do it purposely!" she cried. "It was an accident that he dropped it!"

"So it *was* him—I thought so."

Sylvie bit her lip. She had fallen into that trap.

"It was Timms, too. They were fighting and between them they dropped it."

"I'll go down and see your father now, and young Reg."

"Please, don't go yet. Dad won't be awake—it's early. Please wait until he's about."

"Had a late night, did he?"

"Yes."

"All right—I'll wait. I don't want that young hoodlum to get more than justice."

Sylvie began to pick up the exercise books, smoothing out the rumpled pages.

The young teacher walked to the door, looking out at the stretch of shining gibbers, the sun much higher now. Already the morning was very hot, and the wind was blowing. "At least it's made me make a decision."

"What about?"

"To ask for a transfer. It's what my family—and Myrtle —have wanted me to do for months."

She pulled back as though he had hit her.

"You mean you'll go?"

"Yes. I didn't have to come. I could have had a better school. I was warned that environment could be a wall too high for me to jump. But I was stupid and egotistical— thought I could succeed where others, more experienced than I, had failed. Now I've had enough."

"But a teacher always stays two years."

"Not this one. I'd rather leave the Department!"

She moved nearer to him. "The others never read to us on weekends—like you do—or took us on excursions."

"Well, I don't think you'll miss either of those things— especially the excursions. Not one of you went willingly."

She could have said that she went very willingly, but she stayed silent.

The young man looked back at his record player. He could see that it could never be mended.

"I'll see your father later in the day—when he's sober enough to know what I'm talking about. It's going to cost him a lot of money."

The teacher went out then and Sylvie was alone again in the schoolroom. She stood for a moment or two, then started to set the overturned wooden desks upright. They were heavy, and there was a bump as each one landed on its base, and a loud rasping as she pushed them into orderly lines. She noticed that the lids and seats were badly scored. Someone had gone along them with a penknife or razor blade, chiseling deeply into the wood.

Once again she started to gather up the scattered books, piling them in neat heaps. They weren't as damaged as they had appeared when sprawled on the floor. She picked up the chalks and pencils, and Clive Scott's own books. She noted sadly that some of the covers were broken, and the colorful dust jackets torn. That was a great pity—the schoolteacher was very careful with his books. She remembered that Timmsee had done much to wreck the teacher's cupboard.

With everything in place, the destruction was not nearly as obvious—except for the smashed record player and the mutilated desks. She started with the broom again on the wooden floor, which was permanently impregnated with the red dust ground in by feet over many years. As she swept, it rose in a pale cloud into her nose and eyes, but though she coughed, she swept every corner. Her one regret was that she hadn't swept yesterday. Perhaps he wouldn't have been quite so angry—wouldn't have said he was not coming back next year.

But then she couldn't have cleaned up while the rest of them were in such a devil-may-care mood. They would have called her a galah, and put her out on a limb of her own—and that was a very uncomfortable perch for anyone at the siding.

When everything was restored to almost glowing order, she went out, pleased with her work, yet her spirit was even heavier than before. Mr. Scott was not coming back next year. . . . That was the thing uppermost in her mind. Mr. Scott was going to ask for a transfer. She would never see him again, or learn all that he could teach her. Not coming back next year. . . . Not coming back next year. . . . The words went around and around in her head, whirling like a mill with the wind behind it.

Then she remembered Reg. His trouble was close and immediate—not next year. With great effort she forced the whirling to steady on Reg. He was facing a great crisis, the first phase of which would be their father when he knew he had to pay for the record player. That would make him so angry that the vision of that anger was awful. Besides— where was the money to come from? There was never enough for the ordinary things of life—like food and beer— never enough to spend at the "Tea and Sugar." How could there be enough to pay for a broken record player?

Well, at least she must find Reg and warn him.

## Chapter **Three**

THERE WAS MOVEMENT now in most of the cottages as she stepped out into the sun and into the wind that was whipping up the smaller pebbles. Nearly all the ten back doors of the cottages were open as she went by, even some of the fly-wires were swinging wide. There was the sound of children laughing, crying, hollering to each other; some of the parents were arguing and those who weren't arguing were listening to those who were. There were dogs pushing in and out, and Quinn's radio was too loud.

Sylvie hurried; she knew her mother would like a cup of tea for her headache. As she ran lightly across the slope from the schoolroom she saw the other four playing down on the black rails, Ruby's curls shining in the strong sunlight. They were writing on the cross-ties with chalk taken from the schoolroom. None of the siding children were supposed to play near the railway line, and the four of them had taken the precaution of keeping the shelter box between them and their own cottage.

Sylvie called to the older boy, "Reg—quickly! Reg!"

The boy lifted his dark head.

"Come on!" she cried impatiently. Reg took a long shot with a pebble at the lowered green head of the white signal post, before running up the slope to meet her.

He was not tall for his age, but he was sturdy; shoulders straight, bare tanned legs and strong feet. His eyes were dark, like Ruby's, but his nose was too snub for good looks. When he was thinking deeply, he had a habit of pushing the palm of his left hand slowly upward over the snub point. Sylvie had heard someone say once that a nose like that indicated a fighter; but she found it more comfortable to believe that the bluntness was due to the way he rubbed it, and not because he had been born to trouble.

"What d'ye want?" he demanded.

"That record player—it belonged to Mr. Scott *himself!*"

"Phew-w! Is he mad?"

"Is he mad! Going to make Dad pay for it!"

"Did *you* tell him I did it?"

"No—he got it out of me. But I said it was an accident." She looked at her brother. "Not that it was really an accident, Reg. You and Timmsee were acting so mad—something had to give."

"Course it was an accident."

"Anyway, he didn't believe me—not with all that mess around. He's going to talk to Dad this afternoon, when he's sober."

Reg's brown eyes were worried now. "Dad—and the coppers—threatened me with a sort of orphanage place if I gave any more trouble."

"You should have thought of that yesterday!" Sylvie was curt.

"Oh, we was only having a bit of fun," Reg said uneasily. "Me and Timmsee didn't mean to break the player. What d'ye think we ought to do, Sylv?"

"I've been trying to think. All the time I was sweeping I was trying to think. . . . "

Inspiration lit the boy's eyes and he stood still.

"Why don't we run away! Ain't nothing here. An' Mum

and Dad have got the other three—they wouldn't notice the miss of us."

Sylvie halted too, jolted to a stop. "Mum likes me to help her—give you kids your meals—do the shopping at the 'Tea and Sugar.' "

"But she wouldn't have as much to do if she didn't have us. She always says five's too many—and later on there'll be the new one. That'll take their attention."

"I don't know whether I want to leave Mum." Sylvie spoke slowly, frowning. "She's been a bit sick lately."

Brother and sister looked at each other, both pairs of eyes a little round. It was a momentous thought, and Sylvie was shaken by the fact that her brother should voice the idea that had been in her own mind the previous night. Run away . . . leave home.

Then an angry voice drew their eyes to the cottage.

"Sylvie! Sylvie! You lazy young brat! Where are you?"

"Dad. Not quite right this morning yet. He doesn't call me those things for the neighbors to hear when he's properly sober. Come on, Reg, you'd better help me this morning."

They went warily toward the house, not speaking now, both a little guilty because of the thing that they had thought of. Reg didn't even acknowledge Timmsee's call from his own veranda. Suddenly he wanted no contact with Timmsee.

Their father was heading down the passage to the front door by the time they gained the kitchen. Sylvie was relieved that he hadn't waited to see whether his angry shout had brought her home.

"Set the table," she ordered Reg, "while I stir up the fire."

There were red ashes in the stove from last night and a few dry mulga sticks—brought by rail to the siding from

farther down the line—soon started a blaze. The water in
the kettle was still warm and didn't take long to boil. In the
meantime, Sylvie cut some thick slices of bread and made
toast at the open door of the stove. Reg put out the bowls
for the breakfast food and tipped up the packet. Then he
slit the corner of the carton of milk that Sylvie had brought
from the provision train the night before.

By the time the toast was finished Ruby, Ann, and Billie
had climbed the slope and come into the kitchen.

"Smelled it, did ye?" Reg said scornfully.

"It's breakfast time," Ruby said, "and Billie an' Ann an'
me are hungry."

Sylvie poured a cup of tea and put a slice of toast on a
saucer. "Take that in to Mum," she ordered Ruby; "I don't
expect she's ready to get up yet."

Ruby grimaced. She had been about to sit down at the
table, but she didn't protest. She picked up the cup and
saucer.

"Don't spill it," Sylvie warned.

Ruby held the cup and saucer very steady and walked
with great care across the kitchen, through the doorway, and
into her mother's bedroom. She came back triumphantly.
"Didn't spill a drop. Mum said to tell you 'thank you.' She's
not feeling very well this morning—and won't get up yet."

"She's often sick lately." Sylvie sighed. "Did you see
where Dad went?"

"He went into Timmsee's place just as we came in,"
Ruby said, beginning her breakfast of cereal and milk.

"Wish he hadn't gone there," Reg said, worried; "bet old
Clive's been in to see Timmsee's old man by now."

"Well, you shouldn't have done it." Sylvie was worried,
too.

"Dropping it by accident ain't really dropping it," Reg protested.

"Don't say 'ain't.' "

"Aw-w—what's come over you, Sylv? You've got all sort of grown-up and stupid since this Scott chalk-ee came."

Sylvie went on eating her breakfast without answering. She didn't have to answer Reg when he said this kind of thing. In any case, Billie had just given Ann a good hard pinch on her bottom, and Ann opened her mouth so wide and gave such a yell that Sylvie herself jumped.

Just then their father came in the back door.

"Stop that row!" he said angrily.

"Billie pinched me—here!" Ann pointed to the tender spot. "Twice he pinched me."

"She took my last piece of toast—when I wasn't looking!" Billie's bottom lip thrust forward. "I gotta pinch her when she takes my toast."

"Sylvie—why can't you stop them fighting like this!"

"I can't stop them!" Sylvie flared. "I don't know when Ann's going to pinch Billie's toast, or when Billie's going to pinch Ann's bottom. I can't watch them all the time."

"No cheek from you, girl! You're getting out of hand—I'll have to do something about it. As for you, Reg. . . . "

Reg pressed down hard on his chair when he saw the look on his father's face. The blue eyes were wide open, ablaze with anger.

"What have you been up to in that schoolroom?"

"You knew—everyone knew." It was Sylvie who answered. "You knew the kids were playing in there Saturday afternoon—old Timms poked his head in the door at one stage. I saw him. He didn't tell them to get out or stop."

Her father swung around on her. "Did *you* tell them?"

"No." Sylvie was sullen.

"You should have! You're old enough to have more sense."

"But I'm not too big to hit!" she spat back.

Her father ignored her. Sober, he didn't like to be reminded of these things. "As for you, Reg, it seems you're really keeping up your reputation. Smashed the teacher's record player!"

"It was an accident—Timmsee was in it, too."

"Accident or no accident, Scott told Timms that it has to be paid for—by us!"

Reg pushed down harder on his chair.

His father thumped the table and shouted, "Paid for by us! Old Timms an' me—d'ye hear!"

Reg nodded—his ears were tingling with the words.

His father bent farther in the middle and stared at him, at his level, across the table. "That record player was worth a hundred and forty dollars. One hundred and forty dollars —d'ye hear!"

"Yes," Reg said, and his toes pushed him away from the table. He didn't want breakfast now.

"That's seventy each Timms and I'll have to find. I haven't got seventy dollars!"

Seventy dollars! Reg himself was terrified by the amount. For his father to have to pay out that much money on his account would, even in his own eyes, impose a great strain on their relationship. In any case, he didn't doubt for a moment that his father didn't have that much money. Then where was it to come from? And if it couldn't be got from somewhere, anywhere—what then? What would happen to him?

His father bent lower, spoke slower, his eyes closing to angry slits.

"And there's the matter of those damaged desks—government property!"

"I didn't use my knife on those desks," Reg said sullenly.

"Doesn't matter whether you used it or not!" roared his father. "The coppers know you and young Timms are the ones who always start the trouble."

"You know it too!" Sylvie interrupted fiercely. "But never do anything about it until it's too late!"

"Shut up!" he shouted. Sylvie, as she grew older, was developing a talent for striking at hitherto unsuspected tender spots.

"I reckon it means that the coppers will really take you off this time," Joe Edwards told his son. "They said the last time—after that detonator business—that they were giving you the last warning. They'll put you into one of those homes for young toughs. Maybe that's what you need."

Sylvie looked at Reg's white face. It would break Reg's heart to lose his freedom—to be sent away from home. He deserved it, of course; he'd been warned often enough. But she was desperately sorry for him.

"Why on earth do you have to pick always on the school!" the father fumed.

Sylvie could have told him. It was the only thing at the siding to pick on.

"We'll have the coppers here again in the next day or so," their father went on. "I won't be able to stop them doing what they want with you, Reg. In any case, a bit of time in one of those training schools might do you good . . . seventy dollars!"

There was silence. The younger children ate their toast quietly, trying to be unobtrusive, not part of this quarrel. They watched their father pour a cup of tea and drink it down quickly, and they were relieved when he turned and went outside in a great hurry. But they were not deceived by his hurry. They knew he had nothing to do this Sunday morning except to go again to Quinn's place.

As the wire door slammed shut, Reg sidled toward Sylvie, and when he was near he reached up and pulled her ear down close to his mouth. The words and his hot breath made her eardrum itch. "We gotta go, Sylv," he urged. "No reform place for me—we gotta go. Let's go today."

"Don't spit in me ear," she said.

"Well, I don't want Ruby to hear—you know what a tittler she is."

"I'll think about it. It's a big thing to do—to make up yer mind to leave home."

Last night she had cried to her pillow that she wouldn't stay. But that had been in the heat of a stinging leg, the hurt to her pride in that she was growing up and "too big to hit." She admitted to herself now that the thought had been no more than a thought—an oil to pour over that stinging leg and hurt pride.

But now there were these complications—Reg's trouble, and Mr. Scott. When the teacher found the schoolroom shining clean, would he change his mind about not teaching at the siding next year? What the teacher did next year was suddenly the most important thing in her life. It represented her future. She had thought the future was as far away as the end of the teacher's two-year term. Now, it had suddenly come close. It made her think of the min-min —swaying back and forth—retreating, beckoning.

"I'll think about it, Reg," she repeated, "if you help me find a bit of Sturt pea for the schoolroom."

"Aw-w, Sylv—we might have to walk for miles. . . ."

# Chapter **Four**

CLIVE SCOTT DIDN'T go back to the schoolroom until after the midday meal. It had taken all morning to interview the parents and write the report for the Department. All the families were involved; but it seemed that it was only Reg's father and Timms senior whom he could charge with their sons' destruction of his record player. He was bitter about the record player, and especially chagrined to think he had spent part of his Saturday morning in the Port selecting a new storytelling record by Danny Kaye and two books to read aloud to the children.

The books and the record were still in his satchel. They would stay there. But the real hurt went much deeper.

He remembered those first days in this siding schoolroom —his first school. He had brought with him a fear of his own youth, of being too young, but he had also come determined that his pupils would like him, would feel he was a trustworthy friend, not just a teacher spouting knowledge. Wanting to be liked had made him believe that soft discipline was a teacher's passport to popularity—but it had only made him a soft cake. How they had eaten him up!

He had quickly remedied that mistake and gained a greater respect for the value of discipline. Without being harsh, he became unswervingly firm. With each day's experience he was able to command greater obedience. Soon he was having comfortable quiet in the classroom, and lessons for all grades proceeded on schedule.

He believed he was making headway, believed he was making a success of this very difficult school. He wrote with pride to his parents, and Myrtle. Now this. . . .

What did it show? What did it prove? Only that he had made no more impression on them than a footstep made on the gibbers! He was embarassed to remember his pride. How naive he had been! Even Mrs. Hedges, his landlady, to whom he sometimes spoke of his hopes, must have been amused behind her placid round face.

Mrs. Hedges had cooked a good dinner for this Sunday midday meal, and put on a clean apron. She hadn't mentioned the schoolroom, though he didn't doubt she knew. But it wasn't her business to police the school. She had to live at the siding with the rest of the fettlers' families. She was already far enough apart being the ganger's wife and having no children.

When he had finished eating, Clive went across to the school. He opened the door reluctantly. He hated mess.

But there was no mess. Everything had been restored to order. The blackboard was clean, there was a small piece of fresh Sturt pea in the vase, the floor had never been swept so clean; his own cupboard was as neat as though he had tidied it himself. For several seconds he stood and looked.

He was not altogether pleased. He had wanted the police to see it as it was—to bear out his report. He wanted both pupils and parents to be judged and punished, as much for their own good as to assuage his anger.

It was when he moved that the girl slipped in behind

him through the open door. Sylvie . . . he remembered she had had the broom in her hand. So she had given him time to see all, and appreciate, before she appeared.

He nodded around him. "You've made a good job of it."

She smiled slowly, lips parting. It was surprising that she had good teeth; but then the railways did send a dental survey party out with the Welfare Car regularly. "Things look all right when they're clean," she said. She was plainly pleased with what she had done, pleased with the transformation she had been able to make. Perhaps she hadn't realized before what cleanliness and tidiness could do. From his teacher training, he knew he mustn't destroy her satisfaction, even though he suspected her motive.

"You've made a good job of it," he repeated. "Very good."

Her eyes shone, lighting her face. "You said you were going to bring us a couple of new books back from the Port—did you bring them?"

"Yes."

"Could I have just one look . . . please?"

"No!" Her coaxing tone aroused his anger again. He was sure now that she was trying to placate him, even though he was not certain that she had had a hand in the destruction. But more than likely she had been infected by the mob behavior; in any case she was unlikely to have ostracized herself by setting her face against it. When a community was small it bolstered its morale for its way of life by living in a pack. Sylvie was one of the pack.

"Why?"

"You know well enough. Neither the records nor the books are going to be brought out of my satchel. I've wasted the last shilling I'm going to waste on you."

She was silent for a moment, then she said, "Maybe next year—when I'm better at reading—I'll be able to help you by reading to the little ones."

"I told you before—I won't be here next year. In any case, you'll have to go down to the Port to high school. You should have been at high school long before this."

"High school?" It had never been considered. Her parents had never mentioned it. Besides, though Mr. Scott said she was more than old enough, she knew that age didn't make you old enough. You had to *know* enough to be able to do the work when you got there. The eldest Timms, George, had gone down to the Port to high school two or three years ago. He'd wanted to go very badly and the teacher they'd had then had backed him. In the end, old man Timm-see—who wouldn't let George burn the kerosene at night to do his homework—had agreed.

But George had only stayed the first term. He was not dull, but he'd found himself too far behind those whose parents *expected* them to do homework. Because he was older than his smart classmates, they made him feel he ought to be in a school for the backward. Now he was a motorbike cowboy, a bit farther nor'west, and didn't come home any more.

George had been the last "old one" before her. Perhaps because it hadn't worked out for him, her parents hadn't thought of high school for her. Or perhaps they reckoned, as soon as she was old enough, she should earn her own living. In any case, she knew she didn't know enough to go to high school. She hadn't learned anything much until Mr. Scott came. And he didn't know how she had battled to get her father to agree to letting her continue on at the siding school next year! Her disappointment now was bitter.

"I thought you would be teaching me."

He looked at her. Sylvie. . . . He was sure she would never be pretty. Already there was no color in her face, her hair a tired brown. Her eyes were her best feature, big, green-brown, thoughtful . . . no . . . pondering. Nothing of her sodden parents in her eyes. They were her own. Perhaps the point spelled hope for her. She could be as rude as any of them, but mostly she listened quietly, even asked questions. But she wasn't the kind of child . . . girl . . . that you looked at twice.

"Even if I stayed here, I wouldn't be teaching you." He was brutal. "It's bad enough to cope with all the grades up to the sixth now."

She looked down at her bare feet in case her bitter disappointment showed in her eyes. How angry he was! She wished, with a regret that stiffened and hurt her throat, that she had stopped them. Then he wouldn't have thought of not coming back next year.

"I won't be going down to the Port to high school," she said. "It would cost too much money."

"These things can be arranged," he said. "Anyway, whatever you do, you'll be off my hands." He turned to his cupboard with a finality that dismissed her.

She stood still for a moment before going out the door.

From the back veranda of the cottage Ruby was calling peevishly. "Sylvie . . . Sylvie!" And when she caught sight of her sister she demanded, "Where you been? Mumma wants a cup of tea—her head's still aching."

Sylvie called back sharply. "You're nine," she said. "Couldn't you make a cuppa? I could make tea at your age."

But she knew that Ruby hadn't had to learn because she, Sylvie, was so much older and always there to make it.

As she went across the slope, unmindful of the broken bottles, she heard Mr. Scott tinkering with the door, trying to make it stay shut. She knew it was already shut against her. And although the day was so hot, she shivered a little. Mr. Scott was not going to teach her next year. She thought of the books he had bought and wouldn't let her read. How angry he was. Her eyes were dry, but inside were the tears she cried because he wouldn't let her read the new books. He had always encouraged her before. It had made it easy for her to learn.

"Sylvie . . . hurry!"

"All right, Ruby!" she shouted, and her voice was harsh and strident, like that of the other women of the siding. "I'm coming, keep yer hair on!"

And now she was thinking. How did you leave home from a place like the siding, with waterless country all around? There were only two outlets: the black shiny rails of the Trans-Australian Railway; and the unmade track across to the main road—almost equally unmade—which linked Port Augusta with Alice Springs, and followed the railway for the first two hundred-odd miles.

But the Trans itself was a through train, and she was shrewd enough to know that a girl and a boy couldn't hide out on any of the goods trains that stopped at the siding. Once they were missed, those trains would be sifted for them. In any case, the Commonwealth police and the local police often made a routine inspection of a train. And if they went out by road and hitched a ride on a transport, they would be picked up at the Port, or at Alice.

Reg came into the kitchen while she was making the tea. She knew why he looked down in the mouth. Timmsee was his mate—but not this time. Timmsee was giving him the whole blame for the record player—even said he'd never touched it. That was because Timmsee's father had a heavy hand and a buckled belt, especially when money was involved. She knew it made her brother's spirits low to know that Timmsee had ratted. Timmsee had been his mate.

"We gotta go," he said in a low voice to her, because their mother's bedroom door was open.

"We'll go. I'm thinking about it," Sylvie said. "But there're not many places you can go from here and not get caught pretty quick. Must be the worst place in the world to run away from. Remember that even Old Jack, the Aborigine, says you can't hide out in the mulga—you can go and die out there and no one ever know till they find your bones, but you can't hide. And if we go out by a goods, or by road, we'll be picked up within hours."

"Then what'll we do?"

"I'm thinking about it, see? I'm working it out. All you have to do is what you're told."

"I'll do that, Sylv—I don't want to go to no Home."

"You shouldn't have done it."

"Aw-w, it wasn't anything."

Not anything? He had only taken Mr. Scott away from her, and installed the future in his place. It was this future —this future without Mr. Scott—that made Sylvie decide to go. She had to find out what was to be done with, and in, the future. But there was no one at the siding to ask. Many men came to the siding when life was sour or dangerous, and it was as good a place as any. And the women came with their men because that was the pattern of their lives. The men went up and down the line, retimbering and reballasting the rails that carried travelers across the continent. But it was doubtful if any of these travelers in their air-conditioned carriages ever noticed anything of the siding, unless it was the row of exposed outhouses.

All day, that Sunday, her mother didn't get up. The headache persisted. In any case, Sylvie wouldn't have asked her. She had to talk to someone who wasn't part of the siding, who knew something of another world. And she had already thought of that someone—Mrs. Tucker.

She had met Mrs. Tucker at the Kingoonya Races two years ago, when every fettler and wife and child had gone in to the Races. It was an annual event that was an immense picnic, drawing the people of this large small world for hundreds of miles around. Young Billie had become lost soon after they arrived, and Mrs. Tucker, who was one of the voluntary workers on the fancy goods stall in aid of the hospital, had found him. "Don't scold him too hard," she advised Sylvie. "Little boys can't help venturing."

She had talked to Sylvie as one woman to another who has, at some time, mislaid a little boy. She may have been as old as Sylvie's mother, but her hair was black and soft and wavy, and there were soft folds of smooth flesh at her neck instead of loose wrinkled skin. Sylvie surmised that some would say she was stout, but she thought it was a comfortable look. She noted, too, that Mrs. Tucker never went along to the bar.

She often remembered Mrs. Tucker after that—her cheery smile, her friendliness, the way she made her feel grownup. Last year when the Races had come around again, she had spent a lot of time close to the fancy goods stall. When business had been slack Mrs. Tucker had talked to her, asked her how Billie was getting on, and what other brothers and sisters she had.

And she had been able to do a small service for Mrs. Tucker. By midday a lot of rubbish, screwed-up paper, and cardboard had collected behind the stall's counter. One of the other ladies had gathered up an armful to take over to the incinerator. It was Sylvie who noticed that Mrs. Tucker's red purse, with takings and change for the stall customers, was caught up in the rubbish into which it had fallen from the piled-up counter. Mrs. Tucker was very grateful. "If I'd lost that money," she confided to the girl, "I would have felt duty-bound to make a cash donation to the stall and —to tell the truth, Sylvie—I could ill afford that."

The girl was sure now that Mrs. Tucker would be able to tell her about the future. In any case, she was the only person she really knew away from the line.

When Reg came to the kitchen, she told him her plans.

"Go to Tuckers'!" He was dismayed. "That's a fool idea, Sylv. They'll just hand us over—straight away."

"Not before they give us some advice at least." Sylvie was firm. "Mrs. Tucker is a very sensible woman—she'll tell us what to do."

"But don't you see, Sylv, there's nothing to do except put distance between us—me, anyway—and that training school."

"We're going to Tuckers' first." Sylvie was adamant. "I have to talk to Mrs. Tucker."

Reg picked up the end crust that Sylvie had just cut off the loaf of bread, and began to chew at it. At the same time, he fidgeted restlessly around the kitchen, lifting the lids off the two pots simmering on the stove, taking a kick at the old colored ball that Ann had left on the floor. Every now and again his left palm swept his snub nose upward.

Sylvie saw that he was thinking, and she prepared for argument.

To her surprise, when he spoke it was not to offer argument.

"All right," he said, "what's the detail?"

Sylvie looked with some wonder at her young brother, but was relieved by his acquiescence.

"The Tuckers are on an out-station of Gulla Homestead—north of the line," she said. "There's a goods goes through tonight and stops here in the early hours. We could go part of the way on that, about forty or fifty miles up the line, then strike across."

"It's dry country," Reg said.

"I know. Now, listen. Do you think you could go to bed early, sleep for a few hours and then wake—without making a noise—and slip out to get on the goods?"

"Of course."

"It would be all up if anyone saw us—or heard us. You'd be sure to hit the Magill Reformatory Institution then."

"You might yourself." Reg was cheerful now. "The old man reckons you should have stopped us breaking that record player."

"We'll have a long way to walk after we leave the goods," she said. "Have you got a pair of boots you can walk in?"

"Boots? What for?"

"I don't know—it just seems more sensible to leave home in a pair of boots. I have that pair of shoes that didn't fit Mrs. Hedges—they'll do me. You'd better put on whatever boots you have."

"They're a bit small, and the lace is busted, but if you say so."

"I'll leave a note for Mum and tell her not to worry—it's not as though we're running away proper. . . . "

Reg frowned. "Tuckers or no Tuckers—I'm running away proper. I'm not coming back—not till they say I don't have to go to that school. Do you think it was reform school that dad went to, Sylv? He says he went to school."

"How would I know? Now don't bother me while I think out the note for Mum. And don't be sour when I wake you at three o'clock, or else I'll just go off and leave you to the police."

It was a very short note that Sylvie composed for her mother. But it took some thinking out. It said: "Do not worry about us. We are not running away. Just going to get advice about our future."

## Chapter **Five**

REG WAS WILLING enough to have Sylvie worry out the details of their flight, particularly the initial phases of getting away from the siding. He granted to himself that her years—not her sex—gave her an edge over him. Nevertheless, he was not without thought or plans for the venture, especially as he was not impressed with Sylvie's decision to go to the Tuckers. Of one thing he was certain, runaways should have money for food and such like until they had found some other means of support. Now, money was not an item that the Edwards children ever had in their pockets —or very seldom, anyway. When they had gone in to the Kingoonya Races, their father had given the older ones half a dollar each but it had all gone in one grand and glorious burst at the race stalls held in aid of the hospital. And there was no other child on the siding who would have any money either.

But Reg had a treasure of his own—a convertible treasure. It was two pieces of opal in the rough, with bits of desert sandstone still adhering and hiding some of the glorious hues of green and blue. A fellow from Coober Pedy had given it to him only a few months ago.

He had met the man when he had gone rabbiting one very hot Saturday afternoon at the end of summer. He had been alone at the time because Timmsee had the mumps and was sitting up in an untidy bed with his neck all out of shape. Reg had been some distance from the siding, close to the main north road, when he had seen the man sitting beside a saltbush. The only trees were mulga scrub across to the right. Here there was nothing but faded-looking saltbush.

The bush wasn't more than two feet high, not throwing any shade, but the man was sitting so close that the small salty leaves were framing his shoulders. Reg mightn't have seen him if he had passed a few feet more on either side. The man was hot and dirty and had a swag beside him. He had given one nervous jump when he saw Reg. The two had looked at each other quietly but with speculation.

The man spoke first, in a voice that was raspy because dust was in his throat. "Hello, mate—any chance of a drink of water from the siding?"

"It's a fair way over," said Reg, eying the man with considerable interest. There was always a story behind a man who carried a swag on this road. This man's thin face was dark with short sharp bristles, his eyes set far back as though lurking in little black caves. He wore an old felt hat with a crown like a football, and no top shirt over the gray flannel that reached up to his throat. Even squatting the way he was, cross-legged like an Aborigine, Reg could see he was only a little man. Reg was wary but unafraid as he approached nearer.

"Thirsty, eh? Come a long way?" He spoke as one man to another, an understanding man.

"You're right, mate. From Coober Pedy. Got a lift some of the way—but there's been nothing past for the last two or three hours."

Reg wondered about that. When a truck driver gave a man a lift on this road, he didn't usually drop him short of some kind of civilization. And the truck couldn't have been turning off the road. The only off-track was into the siding, and a truck certainly hadn't called there.

He wondered, too, why the man didn't sit by a bush right on the edge of the road, so that he would be ready when the next vehicle came. Of course, the road wasn't much to look at—just a straight stretch of yellow bull dust, pebbles, and corrugations.

"It's a thirsty country," the man said.

"I'll get you a drink," Reg volunteered. He had instinctive sympathy for anybody on the run.

"D'ye have to tell your old man? Or anybody else?"

"No." Reg brushed the idea aside. "There's nothing in giving a bloke a drink."

"And you won't let on you've seen me?"

"Course not."

"Then I'll be glad of that drink, mate. Here's me billy-can."

Reg had run swiftly and with some excitement over the hot stones back to the siding, pressing the billy close to his side so that anyone in the distance wouldn't see what he carried. It was important to be able to help this man. Plainly, for reasons of his own, the fellow couldn't go himself into the siding.

He filled the billy from the school tank which was not then quite dry, and hurried back, careful not to spill any.

The swaggie was still there, exactly as he had left him, looking very tired, gray-faced. Almost all in, Reg decided, as he watched the man down the billy-can of tepid water, gulping greedily.

"My oath, I didn't know just how thirsty I was," he said gratefully. "And yer ran all the way, too—that was good of yer."

He looked at the boy. "Now, can you make yourself scarce, so that you won't know which way I go?"

"Of course," said Reg, and prepared to move away, happy with his little adventure.

"Wait a minute."

Reg stopped.

"I saw the way you carried the billy—close to your side —so no one would see. Reckon you're a shrewd kid."

Reg looked pleased. He seldom received praise.

"You can have this—the drink was worth it. Saved me life, maybe." From his pocket the man took a worn tobacco tin. When he opened the lid, Reg saw two rough stones inside. "Nice bit of opal in both of those," the man said. "You can have them."

Reg hesitated, in case it was all the fellow had.

"I got other bits," the swagman said roughly. "Take 'em. I reckon you'll keep quiet about me."

"You can depend on me!" Reg promised.

"They'll be useful to yer when you're older. Keep them hid, of course—or someone'll ask where yer got 'em."

"I'll do that," Reg said.

From a long way off came the roar of a heavy engine. "Transport," said the man. "Reckon I'm on my way again. Get going, so that you'll have no idea what kind of transport I traveled in."

Reg took the two bits of opal and turned away obediently, but he was surprised that the man didn't jump quickly to his feet and hurry over to the road. If the vehicle was traveling fast, he might miss thumbing a ride. Then it occurred to him that perhaps the man wasn't going to thumb a ride at all, but wait for dark and a goods train going through the siding. Maybe it was at his own suggestion that the other driver had dropped him at this point.

With the opals in his pocket, Reg didn't look back.

He didn't even tell Timmsee of this adventure. The man had sized him up rightly when he had said he knew he wouldn't talk. He'd kept his ears open for the next few days, listening to the grownups discussing the news on the radio, expecting to hear something of his swagman. But there had been nothing. Over a fortnight later, there had been news of a big robbery at Coober Pedy but this was too late, of course, to have any connection with his man. After a time he stopped thinking about the swagman and what had happened to him.

But he kept his opals a secret. It gave him great pleasure to seek a corner alone, and turn the pieces this way and that to catch the varying lights. The colors were so beautiful, like tiny live flames, that sometimes he could imagine they were alive.

Somewhere to hide his treasure had been a problem. For days he'd carried it in his pocket and then once, while he was running, it had sprung out. Fortunately, he had already developed a habit of feeling for it in his pocket and had missed it immediately, gone back to look for it, and found it. But that had warned him he mustn't carry his fortune around with him. He looked for a hiding place in the bedroom, but soon realized there was no place there safe from Billie's prying fingers. He tried burying it in the ground, on the left side of the cottage, but when he'd gone to dig it up, just to make sure it was still safe, he'd had such trouble locating the spot that he didn't bury it again.

Then one day he'd noticed that one board in the mitered joint of the wooden skirting in the left-hand corner of the schoolroom, nearest the door, had sprung the nails and opened up about an inch. So at lunchtime, while the school was empty, he'd pried the board loose enough to be able to deposit his treasure on the crosspiece of the floor-joist. Then he had hammered the board back just enough to hold it in position.

There the opals remained. They were still there. And now

that Sylv had made up her mind they were going—this very night—it was time to retrieve them.

While Sylvie made their mother a cup of tea and he ate a second slice of bread, Reg looked from the kitchen door across to the school and decided that this was the moment to bring the opals from their hiding place. Mr. Scott would be drinking a cup of Sunday afternoon tea in Mrs. Hedges' kitchen right now, and her kitchen window did not face the school.

He pushed through the fly-wire door and ran swiftly across the stones, hoping Timmsee was also inside eating bread and jam. He made straight for the door, looking neither left nor right. It didn't pay to look furtive. He gave the door handle a sharp wrench but the door didn't yield. He tried again. The lock held. So Mr. Scott had managed, somehow, to fix the lock!

"Blast!" said Reg. His mind leaped ahead to other ways of entering the school. He remembered that a train went through just as day turned to night and would drop some of the fettlers who had been down to the Port for the week-end. They were always rowdy as they climbed the slope to their cottages. He would be ready with a stone wrapped in a bit of rag to break the window on the far side. The noise of the train and the divergence of the men coming home would take everyone's attention from the school.

During the hour that he had to wait he fumed to think that Mr. Scott had been able to fix the lock. Mr. Scott didn't swoon him, like he swooned Sylv. He was just another chalk-ee. Teachers were a pack, and he had never known one he liked better than the others. Only Sylv had some queer ideas about this bloke.

Reg kept out of Timmsee's sight while he waited. He

didn't want Timmsee asking questions or hanging around.

When he heard the train whistle half a mile away he stuck his hands in his pockets and began to saunter toward the school. In his pocket was a piece of woolen rag. He picked up a round fat gibber on his way. By the time the train's wheels were screaming to a halt in the siding he was outside the chosen window—the only one not protected with a fly-wire screen. It was a box-frame window, top and bottom being divided into six small panes each. It took only a second to wrap the stone in the rag, and another to break a bottom pane nearest the lock. Apart from the tinkle of falling glass on the inside, the only sound was a dull thud.

Reg was able to undo the catch and push up the bottom half of the window. But he found even this did not make entry easy, for this window, unprotected with wire netting, would only lift a few inches. As protection against such unlawful entering, a nail had been placed strategically in the frame.

Reg looked at the small opening with some dismay. He hadn't remembered it as being so narrow. But he knew from experience that if the opening was wide enough to get his head in, his shoulders would follow.

A low jump gave him a grip on the sill, and he bent his head to the opening. He had to turn his head sideways, and his ears felt as though they were being rasped as he pushed through. Then a twist, and he was hanging with head and arms on one side of the sill and feet and shoulders on the other.

He almost panicked as he pulled himself forward and his shoulders balked. Supposing he couldn't get through—and couldn't get back! Supposing he had to stay with half of him suspended on either side of the sill until someone arrived to release him! He shrank his shoulders into himself. He used his elbows as a lever on the inside wall, his fingers clawed at the lining boards. Slowly, bruising his flesh, his shoulders edged through and his body followed. But there was no way of cushioning his fall. He could only drop forward, hands outstretched to break the impact. His left palm landed on the jagged edge of the broken glass and he felt a sharp pain.

His feet followed his body, and he somersaulted to an upright position. He didn't look at his hand but went straight to the corner of the schoolroom on the left-hand side of the door. Already the room was darkening. He heard the train whistle and listened to the pull of its wheels revving up the incline.

From his pocket he took the old table knife he had brought with him to lever off the skirting boards. He found he had to use both hands on the knife. The cut on his hand was not deep, but pressure made it sting.

There was a sharp creak as the nails wrenched free. Eagerly he thrust into the dark cavity and drew forth the two pieces of opal.

He didn't wait to nail back the skirting board. Quickly he crossed to the schoolroom door, only to find that it had been locked from the outside! That meant he had to leave by the way he had come.

His hand was hurting and suddenly he was filled with rage against this teacher who made such a thing of discipline and learning, and getting paid—compensation, *he* called it —for damage done to things like a record player. Smart, he was, this chalk-ee. No doubt he'd make money out of this little episode.

Reg was passing the teacher's table, and he gave it a kick so that the inkwell tipped and a black stream engulfed the roll-call ledger and the several books that dammed its run. It was too dark to see what the books were, but he hoped they were some of those books that this teacher Scott was so keen about.

In the gloom he found the nail that prevented the window from opening wider. He tried to move it with the knife, but it was rusted hard into the wood. He needed a larger tool to give greater leverage. He remembered there was a poker in the fireplace where, in winter, an occasional fire burned.

In a moment he was using the poker as a lever on the nail. He had to exert all his strength, pushing upward and sideways. It yielded suddenly, the inner wood of the frame splintering and the window shooting freely upward. He then vaulted the sill, dropping lightly onto the stones below. Fortunately, it was almost dark now. The sound of the train had passed into the distance, and the only breaks in the darkness were from the open back doors of the cottages.

Timmsee lived in the second last one on the left. He could hear old man Timms yelling his head off and all the younger children crying. He thought it was no wonder that Timmsee had denied any part in the breaking of the record player. His old man was a corker at times.

But even this flash of understanding didn't make Timmsee's betrayal more acceptable. A real mate never betrayed his friend.

Reg went into the kitchen with his cut hand and the two pieces of opal in his left pocket. Once on the goods tonight, he would tell Sylvie about his bit of wealth—though not saying more than necessary about the old swagman. He would explain to her that it was distance they needed, not any advice that the Tuckers could give, and persuade her to keep on the train. They would dodge the police somehow. He had no doubt that the sight of the opals—and the security they meant—would convince her.

## Chapter **Six**

SYLVIE DIDN'T SLEEP much that night. It wasn't that she was worrying about what she and Reg were going to do. This wasn't a real leaving-home or running-away—this was just going to get advice about the future. What happened after that would depend on the advice. And if she was going out to work soon, then this would be a useful taste of what it was like to be on her own.

It was more the fear of sleeping beyond the set time that made her restless. Twice, too, she had to get up to attend to Ann, who still couldn't last the night through. Ruby would have to do that when she wasn't here to do it. But Ruby probably wouldn't wake—she slept like the dead—and then Ann would get into trouble in the morning for having a wet bed. Even knowing that Ann would get into trouble wouldn't wake Ruby when Ann called. It made Sylvie a little sad to think about it. Ann was frightened to go out into the dark alone.

She woke Reg in the room next door at three o'clock. He was sleeping heavily, and she had to shake him. He grunted several times very loudly, and the hot smell of his sleepy body came up to her as she stood over him. In the other bed she could see the curve of Billie's rump. Billie was younger than Ann, but he didn't wet his bed. He was a happy little boy, always with a grin.

When she saw that Reg was awake enough to remember what was happening she went out to the kitchen and put the note on the table. On top of it she placed the butter dish with the picture of the Sydney Harbor Bridge. She had put the butter dish on the edge of the shelf before going to bed, so that she found it easily in the dim kitchen. She felt that the butter dish was an inspiration. Surely the Sydney Harbor Bridge would suggest to their parents that she and Reg were heading for Sydney, where—so she had heard on one of two occasions—they had some relatives. It might stop them looking nearer to home, in the beginning, anyway. And she didn't want to be brought back until she had settled her direction for the future.

Then she took the knapsack—the only one they possessed —from the back of the cupboard under the sink. It contained food enough, she considered, for the journey, and a few necessities she had packed during the afternoon while she had had the kitchen to herself. As she knew exactly where it was placed, she was able to get it without noise. Then she went back to her room and finished her own dressing.

She didn't have an overcoat, but two pullovers and a cardigan, all tight-fitting, would keep out the bite of the night air. When Reg joined her at the door, also wearing all his woolens, they went out together and down the steps. At the bottom, Sylvie stooped to take two canvas water bags from their hiding place under the steps. She had filled the water bags from the kitchen tap, kept running with the water brought to the siding by rail tanker, and hidden them there just after dusk. She handed one to Reg, and then they went on through the gate that always stood open. Both were carrying their footwear.

Sylvie was not nervous that Dad or Mum would get up to know what was going on. Neither she nor Reg had spoken a word, and the few little noises were no more than those their parents were used to hearing when they moved about in the night.

They walked down the slope to the line. If the goods was on time, it shouldn't be long. This was a slow goods, stopping at many of the sidings to unload either tools and materials for the railway gangs, or else parcels for the sheep properties along the route. Sylvie planned to leave the train another two stops ahead, at a siding from which a track led into Gulla Tank, an out-station of Gulla Homestead, where the Tuckers lived. They would be on the train about an hour.

The moon was already low on the horizon. Above their heads was a patch of stars that swept down in an arc in front of them. Behind was heavy blanketing cloud. It was an immense vastness, and the darker line where earth met sky was the rim of the world. If Sylvie turned slowly on her heel she could see the whole of that unbroken rim. She felt no bigger than the tiniest cold pebble her bare toe kicked against.

Reg had little to say. He shivered in the night air, and she knew he was thinking longingly of his warm bed and the adverse fate that was forcing him into this night. At the bottom of the slope they sheltered behind a pile of timbers and waited for the first droning sound of the train. It came sooner than Sylvie had expected.

"Come on," she said, and began to run swiftly along the track to a spot which she knew would be level with the last third of the goods. "Dive for an open wagon!" she cried. "Don't look round to see what I'm doing—just climb in. I'll be doing the same. And be ready to hop out again when we stop the second time. Don't go to sleep! And don't get carried on!"

"We must . . . get into . . . the same wagon," Reg said between breaths, "so's . . . we can talk."

The goods screamed down on them. The big diesel sounded as though it hated to shut off the pulsing power and grind to a stop. There were some open wagons in the lead, and then one all-weather van after another passed them. Sylvie gazed with dismay at the latter's bulky gliding shadows. No possibility of getting into one of those enclosed vans! And no chance of reaching those in front now without being seen!

She had almost given up hope when, as the wheels stopped, an open wagon drew alongside.

"Quick!" she ordered. "This is our chance!" She knew that the goods didn't linger. Just enough time to discharge the freight and on again. She saw Reg jump for the nearest corner of the wagon and leaped to the opposite end herself. It was easier to climb aboard from the buffers. Even so, the knapsack—with the water bag attached temporarily—became a great weight on her shoulders. Her right hand had to keep a grip on her shoes and help her to climb at the same time. As she climbed, she hoped that the wagon wasn't overladen, and that she and Reg would be able to be together once aboard.

But this hope was quickly dispelled. It was a very full wagon. It was packed with big wooden crates that stood almost level with the rim. For a dreadful moment, Sylvie could not find space anywhere to squeeze down between them. The thought of traveling full-length on top of the freight terrified her. The goods would probably travel at fifty miles per hour!

Then, in the offside corner, she found room. It was just big enough for her to crouch down with her knapsack. Fearfully, she hoped Reg had found a space too. As the train started to roll again, Sylvie shouted to him, but received no answer above the grinding wheels. The clang and mating of the buffers shook her, and jostled her against the wagon's steel end. Her bare legs were grazed by the crates she crouched against.

As the train gathered momentum, the cold wind of speed rushed in on her. The closeness of the hole could not keep it out. It whipped into her eyes, thrust down the back of her neck, made the sweaters she wore paper-thin. She shivered in her black corner, bent her head, and the wind raced around and above her, vying with the wheels to scream in her ears.

The noise was so great she was sure that the wagon was falling apart and, for one moment of panic, she tried to stand up. Then she steadied. Steel walls did not fall apart, and the further she crouched down in the darkness, the less the wind could strike her.

She wondered how Reg was faring; prayed that he, too, had found a corner. One thing was certain; they could not reach each other against this wind. At least he would not go to sleep in the noise and cold. But surely no other hour would ever seem as long!

After the reprieve of the first stop and start, she was desperately alert for the second stop. It came at last. As soon as she felt the slackening of speed, she eased her stiff cold limbs upright and was peering over the top as the wheels stopped rolling. She wasted no time. One leg over the side followed by the other, and she dropped awkwardly to the ground, knapsack and water bag bobbing up to thump the back of her head, shoes still in her hand. She was relieved to see the shadow of Reg drop thirty feet away.

There was nothing here to hide behind, and they both crouched beside the track, thankful that there was no unloading from their wagon and that the voices of the guards remained distant.

Then the wheels started to turn again and with a screech to the loneliness, the goods went on its way across a continent. Stiffly, they stood up.

"That was a cold ride, Sylv," Reg said, subdued.

Here the ground was as flat as any blackboard, and as they stamped their feet and rubbed their arms, they watched the last winking light of the train until it fell over that rim of the world. Silence closed in on them. There were no cottages at this siding, so there were no people and no inquiring barks of dogs. Not even a dingo would howl in this vastness, for the dog fence across half the state was still further west and kept him out; if he did burrow under it he would never get this far—a dogger would catch up with him. There was not even the sleepy cheep of a ground bird. There were just the two of them.

They stood together, aware of the loneliness. "We've five miles to walk along this rail track to Gulla siding and the turn-off that'll take us to Gulla Tank and Mrs. Tucker," Sylvie said.

"Don't know why this goods couldn't stop at Gulla siding —it stops most places," Reg complained. He was cold, stiff, and irritable. He had expected that hour in the darkness to be sufficient to convince Sylvie that it would be stupid and dangerous to go to the Tuckers. When he had found he couldn't reach her, he had realized that he would have to leave the goods at the second stop with her. For one thing he couldn't have her worrying what had become of him, whether he had gone to sleep or whether he had fallen under the wheels; and, for another, he couldn't let her walk the thirty-five miles of lonely track to Gulla Tank alone. He would have to see her safely that far. She was older, but he was a man.

One thing he did decide in that hour of darkness—he

wouldn't, at this stage, disclose he had the opals. He would wait and see what developed. They might prove a useful lever later on.

"It isn't likely that anyone would think of us getting off a goods here," Sylvie said, "but, just the same, we'd better not leave any tracks for the black-tracker from Tarcoola to pick up."

"Old Knobby isn't with the Tarcoola cops now," Reg reminded her. "They threw him out last year when he got old and his eyesight bad."

"They got another one . . . younger," Sylvie said.

"Well, how are we *not* going to leave signs?"

"Each walk on a rail, of course. You're pretty good at playing Blondin."

"Well, I've had some practice," Reg agreed comfortably. "It's always narked Timmsee that he couldn't balance or stay on a rail as long as me."

"Then let's get going. We won't be able to stay on the rails very far—but even a short distance will help."

They started off, each so intent on their feet and the shadowy rails that led in the wake of the train that it was some time before they spoke.

"We're not the first to try walking on the rails," Reg said at last, warm and cheerful again. "There was that bloke that escaped from the lock-up last year. Old Knobby trailed him for ten miles. Never missed a spot where the fellow overbalanced and put a foot on the ballast to steady himself."

"I've just done that!" Sylvie snapped, vexed with herself and the darkness that was making it difficult to place each foot accurately. "Maybe we could go on to the sleepers now, Reg. Doesn't seem to be as much metal over them as usual."

"Walking on the rails is too slow, anyway," Reg agreed,

finding it as difficult as Sylvie to keep his balance in the gloom. "Didn't you say we have to make the turn-off by daylight?"

"We gotta," Sylvie said. "There's another train through from the west about six. We can't afford to be seen."

"Then let's try the sleepers," Reg said.

It was much easier stepping from one cross-tie to the next, but very monotonous.

"Wish these sleepers weren't so far apart," Reg sighed; "have to stretch to make the distance. Wish . . . "

"Stop wishing!" Sylvie was curt.

"All right—don't bark. How long do you think it'll take us to get to Tuckers'?"

"We should reach there tomorrow night."

"Did you bring plenty to eat?"

"Enough to make this knapsack heavy. But we'll have to go easy on the water. One water bag each isn't much."

"D'ye think we're likely to get lost, Sylv?"

"No. The track in from the siding is pretty plain. I don't know why—but me and Mrs. Tucker talked about that track."

"Would have been better if we'd set out for Sydney," Reg grumbled; "could have gone all the way by train."

"Wouldn't have got any farther than the Port—a few hours away. Just far enough and long enough to make Dad as angry as a bee in a bottle."

"He's that now."

"Well—two bees."

"Five miles is a long way—stepping it out like this."

Sylvie knew it was a long way, but only part of the whole journey. "Aw, shut up," she said.

"Why did we bring the boots, Sylv? Doesn't look as though we'll be wearing them. Let's chuck 'em."

"Can't do that—they'd be evidence to show that we'd passed this way. No, we have to keep carrying them. In any case—who knows?—we might need them when we get to Tuckers'."

They strode silently after that, a rhythm in the long steps that took them from timber to timber. Just before dawn the darkness and silence were heavy. They were cheered when some ground birds, plovers perhaps, chirped sleepily. The sound seemed loud as they sped by.

"Get a move on, Reg," Sylvie said. "If we don't make Gulla Tank siding by daylight, there's not even a saltbush big enough for us to hide behind. I wouldn't like to have to face Dad *this* morning."

They were walking west, but every now and again Sylvie looked back over her shoulder at the rising sun.

The sun did not roll up in a great burning ball this morning. It came with its face veiled—not heavily, but with the cloud thick enough to subdue that first leaping blaze and to streak the saffron and scarlet sky with patches of flat black. Yet it was an angry sunrise, as though the sun were trying to snatch the black cloud from its face and only succeeding in tearing it. And when the first early crimson began to fade, the cloud-black triumphed and smothered the sun in a gray blanket.

"Glad the sun isn't full," Reg said. "I'm hot as fire—could drink the water bag dry now."

"We'll get a drink at the tank at the siding," Sylvie said, "and save our water bags. It could get very hot later. Do let's hurry."

Now that it was light, they began to run along the ties, their hard-muscled legs not yet weary. Except for a wedge-tail eagle that spiraled overhead and seemed to follow their course lazily, they saw no other life. But they were used to vast distances where nothing moved, and the rhythm of their running continued until they came to the siding. There was a tank here and a high oblong pile of crushed rock ready to be used as ballast. They sat on the far side of the stones and Sylvie opened her knapsack and gave Reg a bread and jam sandwich.

"Plum jam," Reg said crossly. "Why didn't you use the melon, Sylv—better than plum."

They had only been sitting for a few minutes when the Transcontinental from the west went through. The long train with a diesel-electric locomotive at either end rushed past at sixty miles per hour. It had already traversed the three hundred miles of "long straight"—the longest stretch of completely straight railway line in the world—but the track deviated so little that its speed remained unaltered.

Peeping from behind the road metal, Sylvie and Reg watched the rear observation car and the passengers standing at the windows growing smaller. The people were looking upward at the eagle.

"Only thing for them to look at," Reg said, unhappy inside because he wasn't on a train speeding away.

"Just as well they couldn't see *us*," said Sylvie. "Now let's get a drink."

They had a drink from the tank and the water tasted dusty. Then it was time to go.

"Couldn't we hide our boots somewhere here?" Reg said.

"No, indeed—can't leave any clues. In any case, this is where we put them on. Won't leave such a deep impression as bare feet."

The track was clear enough here. It led away at right angles from the siding in a wavy line toward a patch of mulga a mile away. It was curly because this was crab-hole country and sometimes a weak spot developed on the track and vehicles had to go around it. Sylvie knew that they must follow each curve faithfully—to take what seemed to be the general direction was dangerous. The track alone, every curve of it, could lead them to the Tuckers'. To try to by-pass it could lead them to their deaths.

The track was mainly sandy gravel with the gibbers stretching away from the edges.

"We'll walk on the stones," Sylvie said. "Our footmarks won't show."

Sylvie led the way. They didn't talk very much. Reg was sure that it was foolish to stay so near to home—proper running away meant putting real distance between yourself and trouble. He wished he'd talked it out with Sylvie before they left. But the decision had been made so quickly there hadn't been much time to think it out. He had a feeling of being trapped. Now, what was going to happen if the Tuckers' advice was to pack them straight back? Reg knew what he was going to do if this happened. Somehow he would strike out on his own—go to Sydney.

Sylvie, too, was wondering about the Tuckers, wondering if Mrs. Tucker would be angry with her for seeking her advice.

And while they walked the sun climbed higher and stronger and soon the gray blanket of cloud was burned away.

Sylvie looked up at the sun and wished it weren't so brazen.

## ♔

# Chapter **Seven**

CLIVE SCOTT WAS not surprised when he saw Joe Edwards coming across the slope to the school, Ruby, Ann, and Billie trailing behind. It was still early. Clive hadn't had his breakfast yet but he'd come across to the school after finding the note on the floor just inside his window, close to his bed. It had rolled almost under the bed and he shuddered to think what Mrs. Hedges would have said if she had found it when she was sweeping the room, instead of him. He had put it straight into his pocket and come across to the school to think things out.

The note said: "If I don't see you again—though I don't think this really means I won't be back—I just want you to know how sorry I am about the schoolroom and the record player. It wasn't you it was done against—just something that gets into the kids now and again. You're the best teacher we've had—the only one who ever bought books and records for us. I would like to have read those books you brought back from the Port. I thought you liked us. But I guess I can't blame you for not liking us now."

The note deepened Clive's sense of failure. If the destruction had been done against *him*, personally, it would have meant he had at least aroused some feeling by his teaching, even if only animosity. But if they had done this thing just because something had got into them—something that would only be appeased by taking a kick at the nearest object of authority—then he hadn't touched them at all! And he alone knew how he had tried—even after they'd shown no interest in his geography excursions, nor wanted to sit quietly while he played his records or read *Wind in the Willows*. At least, all except Sylvie. She had been attentive. But even she had stood by while they did the weekend's damage.

The whole thing was a knock-out blow to his teaching confidence. That's why he wouldn't stay on at the siding. No man wanted to be reminded for an endless number of days of a failure, or, for that matter, go on living with it.

As soon as he unlocked the schoolroom door and stepped inside, he saw the open window. He strode across the room and looked down at the broken glass, saw the splintered sash frame, estimated that it would probably mean a whole new window. He took a quick look outside, noting the bit of rag still wrapped around the big smooth stone. He turned slowly to survey the rest of the schoolroom. Then he noticed the black pool of ink and the two books that had soaked up the blackness for half their length.

His face flushed as he stood at the table looking down at the destruction of the two new books that he had bought in the Port that weekend—the ones Sylvie had begged him to let her read. He had taken them up to the school-room after Sunday afternoon tea with Mrs. Hedges, and there read quietly the chapter he would read to the class tomorrow. At least that is what he had intended.

It was Sylvie's cleaning of the schoolroom that had made him change his mind about reading the books—made him feel that it was spiteful to withhold them. He had left them on the desk because he had believed the schoolroom safe now from attacks, though he had taken the precaution to lock the door and remove the key.

Now the books were ruined! Who had done this thing to

him? Sylvie . . . who had written the note? No—he couldn't think it was Sylvie.

It was then he saw Joe Edwards coming across the slope —the three youngest children trailing behind—and knew that his note *was* from a runaway. Immediately he felt guilty. He was sure, because of the note, that he had something to do with Sylvie's running away. But what had he said to her to make her do such a thing? Try as he might he could think of no reason.

Because the feeling of guilt persisted, and because he couldn't be sure who it was who had done this further damage, he stepped forward, keeping himself between the table and the door.

Joe Edwards was quite sober when he entered the schoolroom. More than ever this morning, he looked hollow in the middle.

"They're gone—the pair of them," he said flatly.

"Who's gone? What d'ye mean?" The young schoolteacher spoke sharply and crumpled the note in the pocket of his jeans.

"Sylvie and Reg. Sometime in the night—on one of the goods, I suppose."

"They've run away?"

"Yes—left a note to say that they were going to get advice about the future. I don't know what that means."

"Probably frightened of the inquiry they knew would be held about the damage to the schoolroom."

"You've already notified the police?"

"Yes."

"Pretty quick, weren't you?"

"This sort of thing has to be dealt with immediately, Mr. Edwards," Clive Scott said. "These youngsters have to realize that they must have respect for other people's property, government and private."

Joe Edwards looked around the schoolroom. "Doesn't look too bad now," he said.

"Sylvie cleaned it up." Clive didn't add that he had been annoyed about the cleaning-up before the police could get there. He had been angry enough to want to see both children and parents taught a lesson by the law. Now there would be the window to be investigated, but in the meantime he was going to make no accusations until he was sure.

The young man and the older man each waited for the other to say more. Clive looked down at his shoes, noticing how the upper leather was scored with constant walking on stony ground. Joe Edwards rubbed a calloused hand around and around a stubbly chin.

Billie sat down at one of the desks and began to explore the recess under the lid. The things he could feel in its depths intrigued him and he lay flat on his stomach along the seat, peering in, arm outstretched, his short denim pants faded on the seat. He grunted as he began dragging out the exercise books, torn readers, pencils, a heap of quandong stones. When the whole contents of the desk tipped forward onto the floor Ruby frowned and rushed to her little brother.

The magnitude of the fuss, her father voluntarily interviewing the teacher, Sylvie and Reg not being there at breakfast—it was all a little incomprehensible to her, even though she had been in the schoolroom fracas. But at least she recognized that authority had taken sufficient battering, and a littered schoolroom floor was another batter. She attacked her little brother with enthusiasm, dragging him by the heels from the desk so that the top end of him landed on the floor.

He was a shrewd little boy, used to protecting himself from his older family, and he put out his hands to save the tip of his nose. His hands took the weight of the fall and stung a bit, but it was the ignominy of his position—face downward on the schoolroom floor in front of the teacher— that hurt his dignity. He lay as he fell, making no attempt to raise anything but his voice to the ceiling, at the same time beating his bare feet on the wooden floor.

"You're a naughty boy," said Ruby, and wondered if she were strong enough to set him on his feet, as Sylvie would have done.

"Don't yoo-hoo," said Ann, and poked him with her big toe in the ticklish part of his groin. He twitched with the tickle and yelled louder.

His father stepped forward and stood the little boy on his feet. The redness of Billie's face flooded up into the skin under his flaxen hair, turning it pale pink; his blue eyes—as blue as his father's—disappeared behind a fringe of long yellow lashes and tears. Ruby looked at the teacher. Why didn't he do something about Billie's awful noise?

But Clive was thankful that Billie was pre-school age.

Joe Edwards took his son by the shoulders, thrust him outside the schoolroom door, and hissed at his daughters. "Get out of here! Why the hell you had to follow me, I don't know!"

Ruby's face dropped into a heavy sulk. She had only been trying to help, to do what Sylvie would have done. Ann followed her out the door with a nervous giggle. While this kind of fireworks was exciting, it was frightening, too.

The incident had wiped away any diffidence Joe might have had when he first confronted the schoolteacher. Now, hands low on hips too bony to hold his trousers at waist level, his head a little on one side, eyes wide open, he lifted his chin aggressively.

"Have *you* any idea where they might have gone?"

"No," Clive said.

"I thought Sylvie might have said something to you . . . sometime. That's if this notion has been brewing in her mind. I know she set great store on your learning—thought you were rather special as a teacher. The way she nagged to be able to stay on at school next year!"

Clive felt his face getting hotter.

"Did she ever talk about wanting to go to some other place—ever talk about wanting to leave home?" Joe leaned forward from the waist, looking straight at the teacher.

"No . . . not to me."

"I don't know where to begin looking." The blue eyes were beginning to hide again behind the loose lids.

"You'll have to go to the police, Mr. Edwards."

"Police! At this stage?"

"Well, the sooner they're notified, the sooner your children will be found."

"Yes—I see that point. But if we could find them first—and hush it up—it would be better for everyone, I reckon. The police pry too much—want to know too many things about a bloke."

"They'll be here today, anyway, about the school. . . . "

"Yes—but that's different. Not as personal as their running away from home. All the kids are in trouble about the school. Of course, I know Reg and young Timms are in special trouble about the record player. But this running away—they're going to ask *me* a lot of questions. They'll expect *me* to know why they ran away."

"Well, have you any ideas?"

"Not really. I did give Sylvie a clip on the legs the other night—but she's used to me doing that when I've had a few. I reckon that wouldn't make her go. Did she tell you about that?"

"No, Sylvie doesn't tell me things like that. She's loyal to her family, Mr. Edwards."

"Guess she is. The thing that's worrying me is that they might want to take her too—and put her in some kind of reformatory."

"Sylvie doesn't need a reformatory!" Clive said violently.

"Well, perhaps not a reformatory—but you know what I mean—take her away from home."

Clive saw what Joe Edwards was afraid of. That prying welfare officers might think it better for Sylvie if she were taken out of her present environment.

"The last time young Reg was in trouble, the police threatened he would have to go . . . " Joe Edwards said. "It'll break up their mother, of course."

Clive looked back at the man—hollow in the middle, graying black hair, eyes still the same color as Billie's. Perhaps they had once been laughing, cheeky eyes, too—a long time ago. Clive couldn't make up his mind just what Joe Edwards' feelings were at this moment—whether it was concern for the whereabouts of his children, concern for their future, concern about the police prying, concern for his wife—that had prompted him to seek the young schoolteacher's advice.

Joe Edwards turned to the door, then swung half back. "Then you think it'll have to be the police right away?"

"I do, Mr. Edwards."

The man shut his lips hard on the sigh that came up from the hollow. "All right—I'll get Hedges to put a call through to Kingoonya. The little blighters!"

He jumped the couple of steps down to the stony ground, and a few yards down the slope was trailed again by Ruby, Ann, and Billie, who had been listening outside the schoolroom window.

"Sylvie's run away," Clive heard Ruby explaining to the two smaller ones. "You'll have to get up at night on your own now, Ann. I'm not going to creep out in the dark with you every night of my life!"

Ann started to cry then, and the sound was loud on the morning air.

Clive started down the hill after them. He felt it would be just as well if he heard what Joe Edwards told the police at Kingoonya. He was suddenly sorry for Sylvie. He didn't know much about the law, but he realized that many people, especially such people as welfare officers, might think that there were better places than the siding for a girl like Sylvie. But he also knew that even if Sylvie had run away, she was very attached to her family.

He saw Joe Edwards, followed by the three children, turn in at Hedges' gate. He wondered what Joe Edwards had done to make him dislike the idea of prying from the police.

At the door, Edwards turned and flung the words back at the schoolteacher. "I love my kids—don't make any mistake about that!"

Clive Scott was glad then that he hadn't mentioned the ink and the ruined books. He made·up his mind to eat his breakfast quickly and get the mess cleaned up before the police arrived. As for the window—he had no alternative but to report the breakage. But he comforted himself with the thought that the culprit could have been any one of the siding children.

❦

# Chapter **Eight**

SYLVIE AND REG walked quickly through the early morning, the mulga scrub beckoning ahead. Here the gibbers gave place to a fine red gravelly sand, and the rutted track wound deeply between the sparse, low trees. Many of them were black and dead. It was two years since there had been a rain, and not a blade of anything green showed on the red earth, smooth between the trees where the wind had swept it. The only green was in the needle-like foliage of the living mulga, and that was discolored with dust; or the occasional bullockbush, eaten back to a neat ceiling as high as the sheep could reach.

They saw few birds. Sometimes they disturbed a flock of galahs that rose squealing in a flash of rose pink and silver gray from the branches ahead. And there were crows, cawing high up, black against a sky that was as blue as any sea scene on a tin. They saw the crows' nests swaying at the very top of the mulga trees, big deep open nests, the outside made of sticks and twigs.

They were a mile or two from the railway line when they came upon a yellow notice board on a post. The writing was in black. It said, *Prohibited Area—Do not proceed beyond this point*. But they did not pause. They knew this was Woomera Rocket Range country—a stretch of near-desert, and some of it real desert—extending in a strip for over a thousand miles across nearly three-quarters of South Australia to the West Australian border, and beyond to the West Australian coast. It was across this country that firings of the rockets tested at Woomera took place. In the main range area only people with a permit, or whose homes were in the area—but who had the protection of air-raid shelters—were allowed to enter.

"They fire a lot of those Skylark Rockets through the day, don't they, Sylv?" Reg said, as they hurried on.

"Yes—that's the one that looks like a black pencil rushing up into the sky, and then suddenly curls and twists like a snake," said his sister. "I hope they don't fire any while we're walking through here—especially as nobody knows we're here."

"It could be exciting," said Reg, and added, "I'm going to take my boots off, Sylv; they're too small and they're making marks in the sand anyway."

"All right, tie them round your neck."

So Reg knotted the laces and slung an old boot on either collarbone. Sylvie took off Mrs. Hedges' shoes and stuffed them into her knapsack, which was already heavy enough.

They walked for a long time through this patch of sighing mulga scrub, and then they came to more flat, bare country and more gibbers. These stones were dark in color and shone like black coal. The sun was high now and so hot it burned with a white light.

They were soon wishing for the sparse shade they had left, and when Sylvie produced two old cotton sunbonnets from her knapsack, Reg made no objection to putting one on.

"You're getting to be a real ole woman, Sylv," he said gratefully.

Soon they were putting on their boots and shoes again,

too. The stones and sand not only burned their tough feet, but softened them up, so that they felt the stab of the three-corner jacks and bindy-eye burrs.

"Now I know why I thought we should bring these shoes," Sylvie said.

But the unaccustomed footwear wasn't comfortable now that they were so hot, for their feet swelled with the heat and the leather pinched and chafed where it was ill-fitting. Their pace slowed. It took stamina to keep walking in this flat desert country. It was lonely, too, even though the track kept unwinding ahead of them.

Reg wanted a drink of water after only an hour in this dry heat, but Sylvie was adamant that they must not drink under two-hour intervals, and then only a few mouthfuls. Only by being frugal would their water supply last the two days, and there was no surface water in this country.

"In any case," she reminded him, "the more you drink, the faster you sweat—and that quickens dehydration."

Reg looked at his sister admiringly. "What a lot of funny things you know, Sylv," he said.

"I've heard Dad say that." And she warned him, "Try not to lick your lips more than you have to."

They walked on, and now they shared the track with all the small black flies of the desert. Their backs crawled with them; they had to beat them constantly from their eyes and noses; they itched where the pests swarmed over exposed flesh; the buzz around their heads became a soundbox in which they were trapped. They walked with heads down, and the movement of their arms became automatic, like that of their legs.

By midday, the track led through mulga scrub again and here they rested for a time and took off their shoes and cooled their blisters. Here, not a dozen yards from them, a pair of galahs lay with wings outstretched on the red earth, beaks agape, panting; in their extremity unafraid of the two young humans who were so near.

"Must be pretty hot—when the galahs look all in," Reg said, swishing still at the flies yet speaking quietly, so as not to disturb the birds. "Wish we could give them a drink."

"We haven't enough water ourselves," Sylvie said sadly. "Maybe in the cool of the evening, they'll be able to fly to a bore."

"How far to the Mungawalla Rock, Sylv?" Reg said.

"Fifteen miles from the siding—not really far."

Not too far, anyway, for their thin tough-muscled legs. This country bred different long-legged sheep from the eastern parts of the continent—sheep carrying up to fifteen pounds of wool that could survive in 120 degrees and more of heat, when the native kangaroos and emus perished. It bred different children, too, tough strong children.

"We'll have done twenty miles by the time we get to the Rock," Sylvie said. "We'll camp there for the night—and have fifteen to do tomorrow; should make Tuckers' in the late afternoon if we get away at daybreak."

But they were long, long miles, stretching to a horizon that, like the min-min, always receded. There was little diversion to make them forget the heat and the distance. An occasional old man kangaroo, resting with his doe and joey under a myall or a black oak, leaped up and away at their approach. The long thick tails, never touching the ground, rose and fell rhythmically with each great hop, balancing the unevenly distributed weight of the body.

"They can do thirty-five miles an hour," Reg said enviously, scuffing his feet as the roos disappeared in the distance.

Or sometimes they disturbed a pair of emus in the saltbush, and the big flightless birds ran swiftly from them on their long legs, with fluffy feather-duster tails waggling coquettishly.

Once they were alarmed by a spiral of dust ahead, a spiral of red dust that rose up suddenly from the track and whirled rapidly toward them.

"A car!" Reg cried, and dived for the only cover—a two-foot high saltbush.

"They can't help but see us!" Sylvie said, and crouched anxiously beside him. Together they watched the spiral of dust advance, until suddenly it climbed into the sky and became a swiftly disintegrating red cloud.

"A willy-willy!" Sylvie said, and stood up relieved, and walked on.

The second time it happened they dropped again behind a saltbush but only as a precaution. At the end of the day, no vehicle or human being had passed them on this track.

For most of the day the sky remained a close, deep blue, and the sun a burning white ball. But late in the afternoon clouds began to gather again on the horizon.

"Reckon there's going to be a rain," Sylvie said.

"Aw—how would you know? It often gets cloudy but it never rains—ain't rained for two years."

"I know, but I reckon it's going to rain soon."

To show what he thought of his sister as a rain prophet, and to take his mind off the discomfort of shirt and shorts clinging wetly to his body, sweat running off his forehead and stinging his eyes, and his feet burning again in their boots, he changed the subject. "Sylv, what do you think our old man did?"

"What do you mean?"

"Well—you know he did something—we all know. Sylv

—I heard the Timmsees talking once—old Timmsee telling his missus that he reckoned Dad had done time once."

"Timmsee wouldn't know," Sylvie said fiercely. She was fierce because she felt he should not know. She and Reg didn't know—not for sure.

"But you think he did?" Reg persisted. He could tell by her face that she did.

"Maybe."

"What d'ye think it was?" Reg was eager.

"I don't know," Sylvie said, her heart heavy, "but I reckon it was something. I heard him tell Mum once—I think she was asking him to go back to Sydney—that there was no place for him or her or us . . . except on the line."

"I'll find out some day," said Reg confidently.

Sylvie saw that he hoped it would be something he could brag about. Reg always needed something to set him a little ahead of his fellows. That was why he had started the fooling with the record player. And that made her think of Mr. Scott, and she wished that all this hadn't happened and she were back in the schoolroom with Mr. Scott reading from *Wind in the Willows*.

They came to the Mungawalla Rock at the end of the day. It was an irregular and eroded monolith. From far off it looked like a yellow-red kelpie dog crouching on the red sand. They saw it first as they emerged from a patch of mulga, and it rose bare and washed by time out of the sand. It was dull brown-red now because the sun was sinking, and the massing clouds were affecting the light. They had traveled through varying dry and dying country—some gibber, some mulga, some myall, a stretch of black pine and sand dune—but now between them and the crouching rock was nothing but a smooth stretch of flat sand.

When they saw the rock ahead, Sylvie said, "We'd better carry some bits of mulga with us—can't see a tree or any good wood over by those rocks, and it might get cool later. In any case, it will cheer us up."

"Someone might see the fire."

"Who? The man in the sputnik? No. Load yourself up, Reg. There's no one here but us."

Perhaps it was foolish to think of making a fire when their brown weathered skins were still scorched by the sun. But Sylvie knew that the fire would be a third companion in the loneliness.

They stacked their arms full of the dead mulga branches and set off across the red sand, still following each flat curve of the track. It was at least a mile to Mungawalla. Their arms were more tired than their legs by the time they reached the rock. Behind them the sky was black now, and ahead was the last crimson of sunset. There was no air moving—only the silence listened to their coming. Close to the track, a hundred yards or so from the rock, a good specimen of dead-finish stood alone.

"There," said Reg, "we could have burned that."

He dropped his armful of wood, pulled off his boots for the last time that day and ran to the rock. Still on the run, he started to climb, leaping from shelf to shelf as an Aboriginal boy might have done, until he stood at the top of this rocky outcrop.

"Reckon it's hollow inside, Sylv," he called down. "Sort of echoes as I jump."

And while he jumped around, pleased at the altitude after the flatness, Sylvie was deciding where they would lay themselves down for the night. She soon discovered the shallow caves made by jutting ledges at the base of the rock. One of these would give them shelter.

Animals sheltered here often; she could see fresh tracks where an old man kangaroo had dragged his tail in the sand like a child drawing with a big stick, and droppings. Perhaps they lay in the cool shade when the sun was burning the earth or came to rest here at night. There was the smell of them, too—like a stockyard smell.

Then Reg called down to her that he had found a rock hole at the top with water in it.

"Water!" Sylvie was delighted.

"The opening into it is very small . . . with a stone covering it," he said. "I could easily have missed it."

"Now we can have a big drink with our sandwiches," Sylvie said happily.

While Reg continued to explore the rock, she broke some of the mulga chips and, having brought matches, soon had a fire burning at the entrance of the shallow recess. With a flat piece of mulga she swept clean the sandy floor where they would sleep, and then she called to Reg.

"Time to eat," she said.

He came down swiftly, leaping light as a dingo from ledge to ledge, blisters on bare feet forgotten.

"Not more bread and jam!" he grumbled.

"What else could I bring!" Sylvie shot at him. "Anything else would have been missed straight away."

The sun on the knapsack had dried out the sandwiches and made them curl out at the edges, discolored where the jam had run.

Sylvie was glad when night dropped suddenly and there was only the fire to illumine what they were eating.

Now that they had finished the day's journey they both realized how tired they were, how their skin was taut where the sun had burned it, how the muscles of their legs were stiff and angry, how their ill-used feet scuffed gratefully in the cold, cold sands of night. Yet they were glad of the small friendly fire, too, as they sat on the outer edge of its circle, and looked up at the dark dome of the night sky. There was still heavy cloud in the east, but directly above them, stretching to the west, the sky was a jewel of stars.

Then, far across the sand, a yellow-white glow on the horizon suddenly silhouetted the black line of the mulga scrub. The glow brightened and spread upward as though someone behind the scrub was switching on one high-powered lamp after the other.

"The moon . . ." Sylvie said. "It's early tonight."

As they munched slowly on their crusts, they saw the moon rise. First just the glowing rim, steadily emerging from the other side of the world until, once above the trees, it looked like the round full yoke of a yellow egg, painted with fantastic shapes.

They watched it climb the sky, gradually becoming smaller and whiter yet lighting their world so that Mungawalla threw a great dog shadow behind them, and the dead-finish traced a lace pattern on the glowing sand.

They had finished their crusts and drunk, without stint, from their water bags, when they saw a new star climb from below the rim and travel steadily across the dome through the maze of other stars, heading into the west.

"Look at that, Sylv!" Reg said excitedly. "Reckon that's the sputnik we were talking about."

Sylvie stared at the small winking star, moving determinedly across the tremendous space. It certainly wasn't a min-min. A min-min wasn't so exact, so sure of its direction —a min-min beckoned, and receded, and when you went after it, taunted you by dousing its glow. This light traveled high and steadily.

Both pairs of eyes followed its course across the heavens.

It didn't appear to be traveling fast, yet before long it dropped below the western rim.

"Must be one of the satellites," Sylvie agreed. "I heard that—if they're high enough up—they keep on going round and round the earth—up there with the stars. And there's a satellite tracking station at Woomera, you know."

They stared into the dark jewelled space.

"You can see everything that's in the sky from here," Sylvie said softly. "Maybe that's why they chose this country for Woomera."

"It's very quiet here, Sylv," Reg said, and his sister knew this was not the tough Reg talking, but the boy who was eleven.

Yes . . . it was quiet here. Now that the movement of the strange star had ceased, there was no movement or noise anywhere but their own—no sound, no footfall of animal, the flies had gone to rest, and even the fire burned without a sound. Yet to Sylvie, the silence was a presence, too, listening.

"This was a place where the Aborigines held corroborees —one of their sacred places," she said.

"How do you know?"

"I've heard Old Jack talk about it. But they don't come here now."

"Why?"

"They're nearly all dead—and those who still lived in the area were moved when Woomera was started. They were sent to some other place where the government said they would be safe from bits of falling rocket—but sending them away didn't make them safe. Old Jack told me they just died, anyway, because they didn't want to leave their country—their place—and the water in the rock-hole. . . . "

"Is that why the rock seems sad, Sylvie?" asked the boy.

"I suppose it is."

"Funny . . . how just a rock could be sad."

It seemed to Sylvie then that all the Aborigines who had loved this spot were there in the darkness, listening to her and Reg talk—that the silence was their presence.

She felt her young brother shiver beside her, though the mulga wood was sending out a good steady heat.

"Let's get some sleep, Sylv," he said quietly.

"Yes," she said, "we must start again at daylight."

They stretched out on the place she had cleaned under the rock ledge. As Sylvie closed her eyes, she wondered if there were animals out there who were balked by the fire from coming to rest in the caves. Perhaps when the fire died down and the two humans slept, they would come in.

The next morning, before the sun came over the horizon, Sylvie repacked the knapsack while Reg climbed again to the top of Mungawalla. He filled the water bags from the rock pool and then, with the sun beginning to tint the rock with gold, ran lightly all over it, listening for the reverberations of his footsteps as he had done the evening before.

The sun was only beginning its climb when they started off.

"It's very hot already," Sylvie said. "We must get as far as we can before the sun gets high."

"You said it was going to rain," Reg reminded her.

"Well, there are still heavy clouds here and there," Sylvie said.

But in that large sky the cloud was not in the same part of the expanse as the sun and, with an early dry wind blowing, they were very hot by the time they had crossed the stretch of sand and entered the mulga scrub again.

Then Reg said, "I left the stone off the hole with the water in it, Sylv—reckon the birds will be able to get a drink now."

"Perhaps you shouldn't have done that." Sylvie frowned. "Perhaps the hole was meant to be covered."

The country on this second day was little different from before, unless the treeless patches were longer and more frequent. But there was less gibber. Saltbush and bluebush grew on much of these treeless stretches. This was sheep country but for their entire journey so far, they hadn't seen a single sheep, though they knew they were here somewhere in the flat miles. They had noticed where the saltbush had been eaten back after the last of the ground level fodder had disappeared, leaving only dormant seeds in the dry earth. They saw, too, that much of the saltbush itself was dead. But the bluebush still survived. Even Reg remembered Mr. Scott having taught them that the sheep-man was thankful for bluebush country. It outlasted saltbush, drought took a long time to kill it, and mutton and wool thrived on it.

Now, every few miles, there was a gate to open and shut where a paddock fence bisected the track. Sometimes it was hard to pick up the track after passing through a gate. Evidently, not long ago, a mob of sheep had traveled this way and around the gates their small restless hooves had obliterated the track. Sometimes it took long and careful searching to pick up wheel marks again.

Sylvie said nothing but she found the moments of searching terrifying. Although they had been able to refill their water bags at Mungawalla they had only enough water, at the most, for today and tomorrow. If they lost the track, they might never find it again and they wouldn't survive without water in this heat much more than a couple of days.

Apparently some of the people who lived in this country found some direction necessary on these flats for, here and there, an old billy-can or a bottle, painted white and hung on an old stump or a fence post, indicated the direction.

The fifteen miles to be covered this day began to seem an intolerably long way. They were thankful indeed when, in the midst of this bluebush country, an occasional myall tree, like a gigantic somber-green mushroom, spread its deep shade over the small toadstalls of bluebush. It was not a tall tree but it was shaped very much like an umbrella with a straight trunk of four or five feet, and then a thick expanse of branches and needle-like foliage. The outback people called it "God's gift to the outback."

The myalls were widely spaced in this stretch of country, and in such shade Sylvie and Reg would rest awhile. At midday they were sitting under one of these trees at the side of the track, eating bread and jam that had lost all taste and was almost as gritty as the hot wind whipping around them, when they heard the distant drone of a plane. As the sound came nearer, Sylvie drew Reg close to the trunk of the tree.

"It's a plane from Woomera," she said. "Look at the R.A.A.F. markings."

The aircraft was flying low, not zooming across the sky as they had often watched planes do from the siding. It wasn't traveling a straight course either, but crisscrossing the country almost at tree level.

"I think he's looking for someone, Reg!" Sylvie said suddenly. "Maybe for us!"

"Us! A plane looking for us!" Reg laughed loudly.

"Could be! They do send planes out from Woomera when someone gets lost in this country."

"But we're not lost—leastways, you say we're not lost."

"No—we're not lost—but we've run away. And they don't know where we are—so they could be looking for us."

Reg poked his head forward to get a better view of the slowly circling plane.

"Keep still!" Sylvie warned. "If that plane really is looking for us, we're for it, Reg! Just imagine what Dad will say if our running away has caused a plane to be sent out!"

"Will he have to pay for it?" Reg gulped.

"I don't know, but in any case he's going to be mad."

Reg's heat-reddened face slowly paled under the sunburn.

"It's like I said, Sylv—we should have gone to Sydney. This little jaunt *is* going to put me into Magill—and you, too, maybe."

Sylvie didn't reply but her eyes watched the plane as it went back and forth across the sky, circling, coming in low. At certain angles they could see the pilot in the cockpit. They prayed that he couldn't see them. Their only relief was that the plane never actually flew over the myall tree where they pressed against the short trunk and, as it kept on its erratic course long after it had passed them, they felt fairly confident that they had not been seen.

They stayed under the tree for some time after the plane had disappeared and the drone of the engine had died away. Then Sylvie stepped to the edge of the shade and looked at the hot track disappearing into the ranks of the bluebush ahead. There was a worried frown on her face as she tied her sunbonnet.

"Perhaps we should have waved—let him know we were here," she said. "I think they—the police—call it 'creating a public nuisance' when you cause search parties to go out after you like this."

"But we can't be sure it was looking for us," Reg said.

"Maybe it was looking for a bit of some old rocket they'd fired from Woomera."

Sylvie brightened. "Of course—that could be it—why didn't I think of that? Well, let's get on our way."

Reg tied his own sunbonnet and followed her into the burning sunlight. As he thought more of what his sister had just said, he began to frown. "Creating a public nuisance." That charge had been leveled at him before—so many times that the police had finally made that frightening threat. Now, suppose the plane *was* looking for them, and they'd let it go on looking, goodness knows what the punishment would be for him, if he were caught!

And more than ever he began to think how foolish he had been to listen to Sylvie. What would the Tuckers do for them except give them up? And yet, with that long burning track behind them, and little water, what could they do but go on?

It was very hard going that second afternoon. They walked now into a gale wind that whipped up the sand, stinging their faces and legs with tiny pebbles. There were clouds still on the horizon but the sun burned through their cotton clothes and scorched their bare arms and legs. The gates became tedious and difficult to open, the track harder to find. Sylvie judged that their pace was reduced by half, and with dry tongue and lips cracking had to resist the temptation, for both herself and Reg, to take frequent sips of water.

But every now and again, even when there was no shade, they had to stop and turn their backs to the wind, because Sylvie felt it was snatching away her breath and smothering her.

Reg found these moments very worrying. He was largely

responsible, he felt, for her being in this waterless, wind-swept waste.

It was nearing evening when he saw a few sheep among the bluebush in the distance, then the mill against the sky-line.

"Look, Sylv—a mill! Maybe that's Gulla Tank."

It was a long way off, the round wheel showing just above the line of myall and mulga.

"It could be Gulla," Sylvie said dubiously, "but we've been traveling so slowly—I don't think we've come far enough yet. Maybe it's just a bore."

They trudged with more enthusiasm now and gradually the mill came nearer, and then they saw the thread of smoke rising beside it.

"That's Gulla!" Reg cried.

"No. I reckon it's just a campfire."

Reg looked alarmed. "If it is we'd better hide—or by-pass it."

Sylvie sniffed. "We can't do either. We have to go on and we have to keep to the track—and it's bound to lead past that tank."

Their pace slowed further. They had one more gate to open on the way, and along this fence ran a telephone line. It was the first one they had seen since setting out yesterday morning. They could hear the wire humming as the two of them pushed a reluctant gate shut.

"That'll be the telephone between Gulla Tank and the Homestead." Sylvie sighed. "I'd forgotten about the tele-phone."

Reg looked at the short mulga trunks used for the poles, his lips pressed together and chin thrust out. "Reckon you forgot a lot of things, Sylv," he growled. "I wish I'd kept on that goods—even though it was going to Perth."

"You'd have been caught," Sylvie said wearily, tired of this argument. "The thing we should have done was not run away at all. You can't hide out or run away in this kind of country—there's really no place to run to. I should have known. The city's the place for running away."

"We could have got to a city," Reg said doggedly.

"We haven't got to Gulla Tank yet," Sylvie said.

They both walked on silently, Reg's thoughts busy with that telephone wire. Every now and again the palm of his left hand slowly pushed the snub end of his nose upward.

Then ahead of them they saw the rough stockyards and the big circular concrete tank. At the side, the windmill for the bore creaked noisily. The track swung in a circle around the concrete tank. If they could have been sure of its direction, they would have flanked the tank and by-passed the campfire which lay ahead. But this was too risky. In any case, they were desperately thirsty, and the little water left in their water bags was tepid. Here there was plenty of water being pumped from the underground catchment, and the fact that there was a camp here meant that it would not be too salty for humans.

They slowly circled the tank, Sylvie licking her lips at the thought of a trough where water flowed. Then they saw a dark woman coming from the opposite direction. On her head, she carried the trussed body of a kangaroo, and two kangaroo dogs followed quietly at her heels. Her bare, dark brown feet raised red dust to the wind, but she walked steadily and with infinite grace. She saw them as they saw her. Even so, she turned aside to the left, to the wurlie of boughs covered with an old green tarpaulin. It was close to the tank, and sheltered by a patch of mulga.

A fire burned some distance from the wurlie. Squatting in the shade thrown by the tank was a very old Aboriginal woman, and a man, not quite as old, who stood up quickly as Sylvie and Reg moved nearer. He was dressed in old black trousers and a blue shirt.

"Aborigines . . ." Sylvie said.

"That's Old Knobby!" cried Reg. "The tracker from Tarcoola—the one the cops threw out."

# Chapter **Nine**

KNOBBY WAS AN old man, but his shoulders were square and his back straight. He was not very tall and his legs and arms were bony like those of most of his race. White whiskers bristled in separate spikes out of a black skin. His eyes were quiet but bright—not filmy with age.

He smiled a greeting and, for a moment, Sylvie thought he had a double bottom lip. Then she realized that it was the blob of tobacco he had been chewing. The black blob rested on his lip while he spoke.

"What yer want?" he said, deep and guttural; and they knew he noted they were burning hot, tired, and thirsty.

"How far to Gulla Tank?" Sylvie asked.

"Eight . . . nine . . . mile, mebbe," Knobby said, pointing with his thumb over his shoulder. "You hot?"

"We've been walking all day," Sylvie said, her voice flat. So they had covered less than half of the fifteen miles— walking from dawn to dusk!

"Good bore here at New Tank." Knobby smiled. "I get you drink."

He led the way to the long trough about thirty yards from the wurlie and with dexterous fingers adjusted the stop-tap so that the cool clear water flowed into the trough. He held a jam tin under the gushing water.

Sylvie had never seen such a wonderful sight and accepted the tin gratefully. She drank slowly but without stopping, while Knobby filled another jam tin for Reg. It took nearly two tins full—even though it was a little brackish—to take the dryness from their mouths.

The old dark man watched them drink with a pleased grin. He knew what it was to be thirsty.

"Thank you, Knobby," Sylvie said. Then she sighed. "Eight or nine miles still to Gulla Tank—and it's nearly dark. We won't make it tonight."

"You stay with us till morning," said Knobby, and smiled widely, showing good white teeth. "You go there quickly tomorrow."

He turned and spoke in his native tongue to the two women, both his wives. The older one, Aggie, looked older than he did and the younger, Betty, was probably not much more than fifty. Both women were clad in ragged cotton dresses and, Sylvie suspected, little else. Aggie looked very tired and ill and took scant notice of the newcomers. Betty was the hunter, with her dogs, for the three of them. Knobby was too old now to run down a kangaroo. Neither of the women knew much English, though they answered to the English names given them by the white people of the area. All three were from the Musgrave Ranges in the northwest corner of the state.

Knobby gave orders to the huntress, and Betty took the kangaroo from her head and laid it in the earth oven Knobby had ready and waiting. There was a good fire burning in the hole and Betty let the fur singe off one side of the kangaroo before turning it over to singe the other. Then she withdrew the animal from the flames and waited until the fire had burned down to quiet coals. The kangaroo was then laid on the glowing bed and covered entirely with hot ashes and earth. There was nothing to do after that but settle down and wait for the meal to cook.

The pale, yellow-fawn dogs waited, too, squatting on their tails, thin flanks throbbing in and out expectantly. At first they eyed Sylvie and Reg warily but with no animosity. Later, when Reg made overtures to the dogs, the smaller one, Rosy, allowed him to pat and stroke her head.

With the smell of singed kangaroo fur making the hot air heavier, Knobby led Sylvie and Reg to a spot under a myall where a chisel and rasp lay on the ground, surrounded by pieces of good sound mulga, shavings and cut-outs of the wood, and a bucket of water in which a small carved kangaroo was soaking.

This was Knobby's art and hobby—carving miniature replicas of boomerangs, woomeras, shields, spears, nulla nullas, emus, and kangaroos. When he had a set finished, Chris Tucker would arrange for it to be sent into Kingoonya or Tarcoola, where it would be sold for two dollars the lot. This kept the three old people in tobacco. They chewed it rather than smoked it, and Sylvie noted that Knobby kept a spare blob handy behind each ear. Reg did much the same thing at home, when he was lucky enough to have chewing gum—the back rail of his bed being a favorite parking spot.

With great pride Knobby showed them the carved kangaroo. He had had to use a forked branch of mulga to get the long slender tail and sinewy back legs in one balanced piece. The outer light-colored grain of the wood outlined these powerful legs.

"Used to carve stockwhip handles once," he said. "Good mulga I use. Used to bury in grave the bits of wood—cover 'em with cold ashes—and leave 'em to season, mebbe for year, before I carve 'em." His teeth flashed a smile, his fine old dark eyes remembered with pride. "Best stockwhip handles in world—never crack," he said, then his eyes saddened. "Not use many horses now—so not need stockwhip."

And he led them back to where the kangaroo was cooking. When he sat down to wait, they sat down, too. "Come . . . long way?" he questioned.

"From the Gulla Tank siding," Reg said.

"That be a long way—if you followed the track," said the old fellow. "Half as far when Knobby goes—like the crow."

"Is it really?" Reg asked eagerly.

"Yes—sometime go across to the line. Sell a kangaroo or a boomerang to someone on the Trans, mebbe. Buy lots baccy then—an' tins dam. Knobby likes dam. . . ."

"Jam, I think he means," Sylvie whispered to Reg's blank face.

But Reg wasn't blank because he couldn't follow Knobby's English, but because he was thinking of that journey back to the line—cut by half.

Of course, he couldn't leave Sylv until she was safely with the Tuckers. There were still nine miles to go in the same heat and the same loneliness—you couldn't leave your sister to go alone. But once she was there—that would be different. It had been her idea to go to Tuckers', and she would have to work out her own problem then.

In the meantime, his mind was busy with ways and means of getting back to the line—fast.

"Who is the black tracker at Tarcoola now?" he asked Knobby.

Knobby's eyes grew stern. "No one. My son—he take on job after I get boot," he said. "But they keep telling him 'not as good as yer dad'—so he leave. He go to Coober Pedy to dig opal. He still there. Ain't got got no tracker at Tarcoola now."

Reg thought this was an interesting piece of news and smiled to himself, remembering how he and Sylvie had balanced so carefully on the rails, and later taken such care not to disturb the road metal on the sleepers.

There was a brief twilight of peace now when the air was suddenly still, and the feel of it was like cool smooth satin on wind-rasped skin. Then darkness came swiftly and Knobby said the kangaroo would be ready to eat. In the light of the fire, branches of mulga with its needle-like foliage were spread on the ground and the carcass lifted from the ashes and placed upon them. Knobby carved off chunks of meat and handed them around, giving the dogs their share.

The meat was tough with a strong flavor because it had not been cooked long, but Sylvie recognized the hospitality and ate steadily, nudging Reg when she saw a critical remark bubbling to his lips. Though the police had no use for the old black tracker now and didn't encourage him and his wives to hang about the town, Knobby had carried no resentment back into the bush with him. He was pleased to share what he had with Sylvie and Reg. So they chewed strongly, and because they were hungry after a diet of dry bread and jam sandwiches, the tough meat went down.

Then Knobby announced that it was bedtime and indicated that Sylvie and Reg could share the shelter. Here again Sylvie did not like to refuse the old man's hospitality. But it was a tight squeeze—five in the little wurlie, as well as the two dogs, who were part of the whole. During the night, the dogs completely overcame their wariness, and slept as close to Reg as master and mistresses would allow.

It was stuffy in the wurlie, stuffy and hot, and sometimes the wind that had risen again thrust the smoke from the fire into the shelter and made the sleepers cough.

Sylvie and Reg were nearest the entrance. They were both aching with tiredness. It had been a day-long battle with heat, dust, and wind. Yet, for a long time, Sylvie stared up at the patch of sky she could see. This night wind was not as fierce, but still strong enough to make the mill rasp as it drew the cool, cool water from the depths of the earth, and to keep the clouds moving in the higher strata. The clouds were heavy again and constantly changing formation, now banking, now revealing the stars, but never clearing to a starry night.

The Southern Cross hung about a third of the sky's arc above the horizon, and in moments of clear view Sylvie stared at it, remembering how Mr. Scott had said you could determine, from its position, north and south or east and west. You used your fingers as dividers, he said, and measured four lengths and a half of the long span to the right, toward the celestial pole, then dropped sharply to earth. The point of contact was true south. What a lot of interesting things Mr. Scott knew—and you remembered what he told you.

Presently she dozed, and immediately she dreamed of Mr. Scott. But in the haziness of sleeping and waking it wasn't really a dream, but a reliving of that moment, a couple of days ago now, when he had said, " . . . whatever you do, you'll be off my hands."

She didn't know why those words made her heart so cold, so cold that she woke again properly, and went on thinking about them until Rosy the dog nuzzled her elbow. There was something so friendly about the dog's touch that she was comforted, and presently slept on the hard ground.

This was the moment Reg was waiting for. Normally he would have slept as soon as he put his head on the earth but, though he was very tired bodily, his brain was extremely awake. He had decided that there was something he had to do before he slept—something that would give him some chance of keeping his freedom. Old Knobby had confirmed that the telephone wires along the last fence and leading on past the tank were from the main homestead to the out-station of Gulla Tank. That line would bring police or plane out to Gulla Tank in no time! And then for him and Sylvie . . . back to the siding to face even more terrible strife than they had left. To be followed with that training school.

The very idea still shocked him. Not that he hadn't been warned a hundred times by Mr. Scott, by his mother, by his father, by the police themselves. But as long as he had known that he still had to do the thing to bring it about, it was far away. Now it had happened.

Well, he was going to give himself a sporting chance of not being caught. He was going to cut that telephone wire! And after he'd seen Sylvie safely to Tuckers', he would return to Knobby, bribe him with a piece of his opal— Knobby would know something about opal, seeing that his son was digging at Coober Pedy—to take him, as the crow flies, to the siding where he and Sylvie had left the goods train. More trains stopped at this siding, and he would hide out there until a goods or a Trans—going east!—stopped long enough for him to sneak aboard.

The more he detailed his plan, the better it seemed. He began to think that the delay caused by Sylvie's determination to go to Gulla Tank might have its advantages after all. At least, by now, they would have stopped searching the trains for them.

He waited until the sound of Sylvie's breathing was heavy, then he gradually eased himself to a sitting position,

then onto his feet, watching for movement from the
Aborigines also. A few steps and he was clear of the wurlie.
Then he stood very still, waiting again for sound of movement, or someone to follow him out. But no one stirred
and no one followed except Rosy the dog. She padded out
on silent feet and waited soundlessly a yard or two away. He
would like to have spoken to her, reassured her, but dared
not make a sound.

His bare feet were as silent as an Aborigine's in the sand
as he circled the tank, the dog keeping him company. The
shifting clouds made it dark, and he had to be careful not
to fall over broken mulga branches, or cut his bare feet on
mutton rib bones. He went first to where Knobby kept his
tools under the myall tree. There he rummaged until he
put his hand on the rasp. He wished Knobby possessed a
pair of wire cutters, but was thankful for what he found.
Then, from the far side of the tank, he located the line of
shadowy telephone poles and followed from one pole to the
next. Once he mistook a straight dead mulga for a pole and
for a moment thought he was lost. It was a moment of cold
panic, for without the telephone line to guide him he could
never find his way back. It would have meant shouting to
rouse the camp, or remaining immobile until they stirred in
the morning, which would have put an end to his plans.

With the dog keeping pace with him two or three feet
from his side, he walked about a quarter mile from the
camp, and decided that he had come far enough. There was
no singing on the wire—the line was dead. The top of the
pole was not more than fourteen feet from the ground. He
had shinned up higher poles than that. Arms clasped around
the slender trunk, the rasp between his teeth, he used the
slightly jutting knots where branches had been sawn off as

footholds, and for the rest he went up the pole as a grub walks across the surface of a leaf, putting forth its head, then drawing up its tail to meet it.

At the top he hugged the tree close for a moment, the rough bark scratching his nose and tickling his legs. Somewhere at the bottom Rosy was sniffing. He hoped she hadn't found anything that would start her barking. Using the rasp, he commenced to saw through the single wire. It made a screaming noise on the night air, and he wondered if the Aborigines' ears were good enough to hear it at this distance. Then he remembered that they were old, even Betty, who was probably very tired after her day's hunt.

The raw noise set his own teeth on edge, and he was terrified that at any moment Rosy would begin to wail.

But the wire yielded to his efforts far quicker than he had expected, and suddenly the rasp bit through and the long length snaked to the ground with a metallic spring. Rosy, tail down, sprang aside to miss the coiling wire but again she did not bark. Quickly Reg climbed down the post.

As he landed, the coldness of the sand on his bare feet sent a shiver right through him. It was a strange shiver—reaching to the top of his head. He turned toward the wurlie, Rosy ahead now but only a yard or so. The wind was strengthening again and turning the mill ever faster and faster, making it rasp and whine in the dark shadows. Twenty yards from the camp, he could see the winking light of the fire. Knobby had put on a big mulga log as he'd gone to rest, knowing that it would burn all night and, in the morning, would be coals in the pearl-gray ash.

A little nearer the fire, Reg stopped in the shadow of a myall, listening and watching for movement. Rosy stopped with him. She was close to his legs now, and he could feel the warmth coming from her.

There was no movement around the fire and so he went forward. At the entrance to the wurlie he eased himself down into the space he had occupied earlier. Sylvie stirred a little.

"What's up?" she asked.

"Nothing," said Reg. "I just went out for a bit of air."

"M-m-m . . ." said Sylvie, and slept again.

But even with the task done, Reg did not go to sleep easily. The coldness that had struck as he jumped the last two or three feet from the pole was still with him—inside somewhere—deep down where even Rosy's friendly warmth could not reach. For a long time he thought about the wire —and suddenly he began to wonder what the penalty was for cutting a telephone line. Earlier in the night it had seemed imperative to do this thing—cut the wire and give himself time to get away. Now he wasn't so sure. A telephone wire was very important. It was a long time before he went to sleep.

At dawn everyone rose, even old Aggie, whose rheumatism was terrible to behold in the early light. She couldn't straighten herself, but crawled on hands and knees from the wurlie to the shade of the tank.

"That why we not travel much," Knobby said, watching Betty hold a full jam tin of black tea to the old lips, with all the love of a daughter.

"Can't something be done?" Sylvie pitied.

"What to be done with old black woman?" Knobby sighed, " 'cept put in hospital place—not her country— where she die . . . dam quick."

The day again promised scorching sun and stinging wind, and Sylvie and Reg set about making an early departure.

Knobby went with Reg to adjust the ball-tap on the water-trough so that Reg could refill the water bags. It was while they were alone together, screened by the curve of the big tank, that Reg intimated to Knobby that he would be returning to the line as soon as he had seen his sister safely to Gulla Tank.

"But it's a long way back, Knobby," he said. "D'ye think you could guide me—as the crow flies?"

"H'm . . . h'm . . . " said the old fellow. "It's long way—like you say. Long way. . . ."

"I'll give you this, Knobby," Reg said, and drew the smaller piece of opal from his pocket.

Knobby smiled with both mouth and eyes. "Nice," he said, "ver pretty. Yes—reckon I guide you."

"Thank you," said Reg, and hoped the old tracker wouldn't see the trembling of his hands as he screwed the corks into the water bags. "I'll try to be back tonight," he added. "In the meantime . . . it's our secret, eh?"

"Yes—course," said Knobby comfortably. Long ago, he had given up wondering about the why and wherefore of what white people did. If the boy returned, he would guide him, and if he didn't—well, it would save a long walk.

When brother and sister were ready to go, the old man gave them some strips of half-cooked kangaroo steak to eat on the way. Having finished their bread and jam sandwiches the previous afternoon, Sylvie accepted gratefully, though doubting the steak would remain good for long in the heat. They would have to eat it before they had gone far, before it turned green. But it would help to keep up their strength.

At the last moment, Knobby gave her, too, the carved kangaroo.

Sylvie's green-brown eyes looked at the old man in wonder. No one had ever given her a present without a reason, such as birthday or Christmas. Even on these occasions presents were not the rule.

"Thank you," she said, and though she knew that the knapsack would become unbearably heavy later on, and would chafe her back, she found a corner for the mulga kangaroo.

And because of the gift she was emboldened to ask a favor.

"Knobby," she said, uncertain whether she was being wise or not, but feeling there was little to lose. "Knobby—if anyone should come this way, please don't tell them you've seen us—even if they ask you to track us."

"Knobby not tell," said the old fellow. "Never seen yer." He spat to show his vehemence and at the same time gave Reg a knowing look.

Betty came and stood in the middle of the track to watch them go, smiling and showing perfect white teeth. She hadn't spoken a dozen words to either of them during the whole time, yet Sylvie felt she had enjoyed their visit—perhaps it would be something for her and Aggie to talk about.

Knobby's last words followed them. "Tell Mis Tucker—be in very soon for tea an' sug an' dam. You ain't got far . . . only five mile . . . that all."

Five miles! That was such heartening news that Sylvie didn't remind him that last night he had said eight or nine. Perhaps he also had wanted them to stay.

Reg's eyes brightened, too. Only five miles to return to Knobby! And if he could persuade the old fellow to travel at night, the whole return journey to the line would be quick and easy.

They tried to be brisk as they started off, knowing that the sun was racing to climb the sky, and the wind, heavy with red dust—the sun's very breath—was blowing ever harder. They were tired from the two previous days, their arms and legs were sunburned, their feet were sore. The five

miles that lay ahead loomed longer than all the miles behind them.

They didn't speak much. Once or twice Reg tried to
whistle, but the wind whipped the sound away and parched
his throat.

For a time their track accompanied a surface pipe line,
leading from the New Tank bore to a trough, miles away
probably. Instead of lying straight—as it had been laid—
the pipe was contorted into the curves of a lazy silver snake.
Heat had done that—heat of the sun when the temperature
was 120 degrees in the shade—and even night contraction
had not returned it to normal. It frightened Sylvie to see
this evidence of what the sun could do.

It wasn't sizzling like that today, but it was getting
hotter all the time, and the strength and speed of the wind
constantly increased. It whipped into their faces, took their
breath, tossed them sometimes almost off their feet. On the
bare stony stretches Sylvie's head, under its sunbonnet, sometimes felt light, as though it were going to float away. She
would hold Reg's arm then and they would stand together,
stiffened against the wind, until she steadied again. They
both knew that in this heat, in this roaring wind, in this
choking dust, five miles was as much, or more, than they
could cover.

At times Sylvie wondered if she would learn about the
future from Mrs. Tucker—or would they be dispatched
straight back home? She wondered what Reg would say if
she told him that the nearer they drew to Gulla Tank, the
more she regretted having ever left the siding.

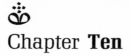

# Chapter **Ten**

SYLVIE AND REG had never seen Gulla Tank—out-station of one of Australia's large fenced sheep-stations, which measured its area in many hundreds of square miles—but it was like others they had seen. It was an old square stone house of pioneer days, built of local yellow-red sandstone—picked up, not quarried, on the property. It squatted flat on the earth, with a wide veranda back and front, screened-in from floor to ceiling against flies and mosquitoes. The wire hid the windows, the eyes of the house, so that it looked as though it were sleeping. It squatted alone on the hot red earth, the nearest neighbor being thirty-five miles away at the head station, Gulla Homestead.

A cane-grass fence, four feet high, protected the house and a small plot of ground in front and on one side. There was no mill here now, but the big circular stone tank still stood a hundred yards away. Originally the house had been built beside a bore. For many years the bore had yielded good saline-free water—fit even for humans to drink. Then the salt content began to develop, gradually growing heavier until it was more than the one and a half to two ounces to the gallon that a sheep could take. Finally the water itself had petered out. In the meantime a successful bore had been put down at New Tank, where Knobby camped, and this water was piped the five miles across the surface to this out-station, and into the old storage tank.

Although there was no mill here, there was the open steel framework of a free-lite reaching to the sky, just beyond the three or four tamarisk trees that grew outside the fence. Its propeller was whirling in the wind, charging the batteries that gave electric light to the house. Fifty yards away on the other side was the air-raid shelter, this out-station being within the main rocket range area.

The shelter was a steel tunnel-like structure, about twenty feet long, with the entrance at either end protected by an outer wall of tar-coated sandbags. Sandbags also covered the entire rounded roof and the sides, which were strong enough to stand the weight of an eighty-ton locomotive. Though weathered, the sandbags gave off a hot smell and remained black and ugly.

Nearer the house was a pen for some chickens that had given up scratching in the stony ground to perch, blinking and gasping, feathers fluffed, on the branches of the tamarisks that tossed in the wind.

Saltbush and bluebush intermingled here and grew sparsely among the gravel almost to the fence. There was a pile of sand stacked up by the wind against the fence. Almost in front of the house was a high heap of mulga logs, a chopping block, and an ax. The only other buildings were an open shed for the Tuckers' car and a repair shed and shelter for the B.S.A. motorcycle on which Chris Tucker rode around the station.

From this out-station, he looked after an area of nearly 400 square miles, divided into twelve paddocks, and carrying 3,000 sheep. His charge included four bores and mills, one being New Tank, with surface pipe lines to storage tanks and troughs in each paddock. Chris had to inspect his fences and waters every two days to be sure there was no break in the fencing, the big tanks were full to the brim, the troughs clean, and the cocks working.

Sylvie and Reg judged it to be nearly midday when they arrived. Reg immediately took off his sunbonnet and stuffed it into his pocket.

As they neared the house, two dogs ran barking from behind the woodheap. Both were red kelpie and border collie cross, but their tawny color indicated dingo in the early breed. Their eyes were soft and amber, and their barking and their wagging tails were friendly. These station dogs were always pleased—as were their masters—to see visitors.

With the dogs weaving around them, Sylvie and Reg advanced slowly toward the house. They could hardly believe they had reached the end of their journey, though to Reg it was only a milestone of *his* journey.

He had suffered a fright on first seeing the B.S.A. standing in the shed. Then he had noticed that some of its mechanical parts were spread on a sack on the ground. Obviously the machine was undergoing repairs. This meant that the fastest and easiest vehicle of pursuit was out of action.

He spoke no word to Sylvie as she pushed open the cane-grass gate, while the dogs stood aside to let them pass. They did not follow beyond the fence, though they continued to bark.

A little gasp escaped Sylvie as she moved inside the fence. In front of the sleeping house was a small square of emerald-green lawn, divided in two by the red pebbled path that led to the wire door. Flower beds edged each strip of lawn— petunias, purple, pink, white; lineria, like a rainbow; stocks, pink and purple; all the colors deep and strong, even though the flowers were drooping in the heat and their brilliance was dimmed with red dust.

Beyond the lawn at the side of the house they could see the vegetable beds. Lettuce, beans, red beet, and silver beet grew in perfectly flat square plots, and though they, too, were dusty and weary, they were still like jade jewels on red velvet. Around each bed was an embankment so that never a drop of water escaped, and not a single weed grew in any of the beds.

"Reg . . . look!" Sylvie had never seen such orderliness, such color, such growth. Unbelieving, she looked from this Eden to the stony red ground, the tired bluebush and salt-bush beyond the cane-grass fence. "Isn't it beautiful!" Some of her weariness went from her in this tonic of color and growing things.

Then a young voice shouted to the dogs, "Quiet, Dixie . . . quiet, Punch!" And a tall boy of solid build, a little older than herself, pushed open the fly-wire door and stared at her and Reg. It was a long stare.

He said, "What d'ye want?" as though nothing could surprise him.

"Does . . . does Mrs. Tucker live here?" Sylvie said, and was ashamed because her voice quivered.

"Yes," said the boy, and thrust his head back into the shadow of the veranda, and yelled, "Mum-m!"

"I'm coming, Jeff." Mrs. Tucker was already nearly to the door. She was not very tall, but broad in the seat and rounded everywhere else. Her bare arms were smooth and full and her dark eyes bright and friendly. A green floral apron, crumpled with constant wiping of her hands, was tied around a submerged waistline, and a red ribbon kept the long, dark, curly hair back off her forehead.

She smiled at Sylvie and Reg. "Why . . . Sylvie!" she cried,

and the girl's heart lost some of its fear. "Come in, my dear
—you and your brother."

Thankful, Sylvie and Reg stepped from the brash sunlight into the dimness of the enclosed veranda. The com-
parative coolness of the stone house was like a caress. They
followed Mrs. Tucker into the kitchen which opened directly
off the veranda.

It was a big, long kitchen but it was very full. Just inside
the door to the left, two small rifles rested in a rack on the
wall; in the right corner was the huge stove where, because
of the heat, the smallest possible fire kept the two big black
kettles bubbling. There was a big wire-covered food safe,
a large kerosene refrigerator, a wide open-topped dresser
with a row of blue dinner plates, edge to edge, on the top
shelf, and a table under the louvered windows on which stood
a two-way radio to transmit and receive messages. On the
opposite wall was another long table on which a meal was set
out. Behind the table, against the wall, was a wooden bench
where two more boys were sitting. Jeff edged in beside them
and the three stared at the newcomers.

Sylvie, uncomfortable because she was a girl, dirty, sunburned, and tired, stared back. Even she recognized that
they were three good-looking boys, about two or three years
between each, so that the youngest was probably about the
same age as Reg. They were solid-looking fellows, with their
mother's dark eyes and curly hair. They were wearing the
bright-colored shirts—two reds and a butcher's blue—the
tight denim jeans, and elastic-sided riding boots common to
the young males of the country.

At the head of the table, carving knife and fork poised in
hand over a cold roast leg of mutton, was a handsome gray-
haired man—not very old. He had a trim iron-gray mustache
on his upper lip and clear olive skin, slightly tinged with

pink. He was wearing a boiler-type suit of khaki overalls. But Sylvie, who sometimes studied the pictures in the social columns of the *Women's Weekly*, passed on to her by Mrs. Hedges, thought immediately how fine he would look in a black suit with tails and a white shirt. He would look even better than the Lord Mayor himself, whose picture she had seen recently. It seemed appropriate that at either side of his chair a marmalade cat was waiting for any meat trimmings, while three more cats of various hue were lined up on the brick hearth.

"Well," said Mrs. Tucker, "visitors—this is nice. Peter, bring a couple of chairs out from the other room."

Peter was the youngest of the three, and he stood up quickly and disappeared through a doorway into the inner part of the stone house.

"Here's a dish of water to wash your hands," Mary Tucker said.

Grateful, Sylvie put her hands, grimed with red dust and sweat, into the warm water, while Mrs. Tucker produced some more lettuce and tomatoes from the refrigerator.

"You look tired—and I guess you're hungry," Mr. Tucker said, and began to slice the meat onto the two extra blue plates that Mrs. Tucker now put in front of him.

They were indeed hungry, despite the strips of kangaroo steak, and Sylvie was especially glad to be able to sit quietly while her face and body cooled and the crisp lettuce and tomato soothed her tongue.

Then Mr. Tucker said, "How far have you come?"

Sylvie hesitated. Only Mrs. Tucker had been in her mind when she planned to talk over the future. She had never given a thought to a Mr. Tucker, or to three Tucker sons. Probably because she hadn't met any of them at the Kingoon-ya Races.

"From the siding," she said.

Mr. Tucker opened hazel eyes under gray brows, and then took another mouthful. "That's a long way."

Sylvie looked toward Mary Tucker beseechingly. There were things that could be talked about only by one woman to another.

"You walked out along the track?" Mr. Tucker went straight on. "How long did it take you?"

"This is the third day."

"Your parents knew you were coming?"

Sylvie stared at the meat on her plate. "I . . . left a note . . . to say we were going . . . somewhere—I didn't say it was . . . Gulla Tank."

"Oh!" Mr. Tucker was very busy for a minute or two with his own knife and fork, while the Tucker boys were silent, listening.

"That means—you've run away?" The question was short and direct. Both Sylvie and Reg knew immediately that this was the type of man Chris Tucker was—direct, to the point.

"No, not really," Sylvie said miserably, and wished Reg wouldn't kick her so hard under the table. "We . . . I expect . . . we'll be going back."

"You had a particular reason for coming here?"

"Oh, yes," Sylvie said eagerly. "I . . . I wanted to talk to . . . Mrs. Tucker. You see, I . . . we. . . ."

"You're in trouble?" Mr. Tucker again looked directly from one to the other.

"Not really," Reg put in quickly, and tried to sound confident. "Sylv just thought she'd like to come out here. Took us longer than we expected. Made good time the first day, though—got as far as Mungawalla Rock. Last night we camped at a tank about five miles back."

"The New Tank—old Knobby's camped there," Chris Tucker said. "Did you see him?"

"Yes," Reg said, uncomfortable under the straight look. And to bolster up his confidence he said with some pride, "I found a rock hole at Mungawalla. There was water in it. I took the stone off the top so that the birds could get a drink."

"You took the top off that rock hole!" blazed Mr. Tucker. "Don't you know it's the only drop of water in that bit of country? More than one stockman has been saved from dying of thirst by that rock hole! The stone is put over the top to stop evaporation."

"Oh . . ." Reg was wretched.

"That stone will have to be replaced as soon as possible. I'd drive out there right away—but my first job this afternoon is to get that bike running again. I have to collect the most valuable of the rams—some of them are worth four hundred dollars apiece. The boss is sending a truck out for them at the end of the week."

Sylvie's first startled look changed rapidly to relief. Mungawalla was at least fifteen miles back—fifteen miles nearer home. How quick and easy it would be for Mr. Tucker to say, "I'll put the stone back over the rock hole, and take you home at the same time."

But he didn't say that, though his next words were just as disturbing.

"If you've been on the road two and a half days," he said, "that plane from Woomera was probably looking for you yesterday."

"It was a Winjeel," Peter, the youngest Tucker, put in quickly. "That's a low-wing monoplane, with a single radial engine. Woomera uses them for spotting bits of rocket."

"Peter's going to be our airman son," explained his father with a grin. But the grin did not last.

"It wasn't looking for bits of casing yesterday," he said. "Flew over our heads too often for that—it was looking for somebody."

Sylvie felt that the food she was trying to eat would choke her. What had she and Reg done! From outside she could hear the wind whistling around the stone house, and the sand and small pebbles rising on the wind to hit the windows. There was a dry hot fury wheeling out there, and she thought of the angry father who had asked, or been obliged to accept, a plane search from Woomera, and who would be angrier when he found them than any fury.

Mary Tucker stood up suddenly. "We'll talk about it in a little while," she said. "I can see that Sylvie isn't very hungry—she would probably rather be having a good proper wash. Now, when you boys and your father have finished eating, you can start on the dishes, while I look after Sylvie. You can help dry, Reg."

Sylvie might have been amused at Reg's surprised look if she hadn't been so worried and miserable. Reg never dried the dishes at home unless he was hounded into it, but these Tucker boys were obviously used to the job.

She was glad to leave the table and follow Mary Tucker. But Mary didn't take her to the bathroom; instead she led the way into her own bedroom at the other end of the house, where she sat on the high edge of the fancy iron double bedstead and invited the girl to do the same.

"What's the trouble, Sylvie, my dear," she said. "Why did you come all the way out here?"

"I wanted to talk to someone about the future," Sylvie said. "I don't know what to do, Mrs. Tucker."

Mrs. Tucker looked at the leggy, thin, developing body, at the out-grown dress, at the uncared-for hair, at the too-old face.

"To do about what?" she prompted gently.

"Mr. Scott's not going to teach me any more!" Sylvie blurted out.

"Mr. Scott—Clive Scott?" Mary Tucker had met the young schoolteacher on two occasions. The northwest of South Australia was a great sprawling area of country, but so sparsely populated that residents often went hundreds of miles to community gatherings. Because of this, she had met Clive Scott for the first time at this year's Kingoonya Races, where, two years ago, she had first met Sylvie; the second meeting with the schoolteacher was at "open day" in the usually closed "village" of Woomera.

She remembered Clive Scott as a well-set-up young man with broad shoulders, serious brown eyes, and a smile that was not frequent but a flash of light when it happened.

"He said . . . even if he stayed on . . . he wouldn't teach me next year. I'd have to go to the Port to high school." There was hurt—without understanding—in the wide eyes. "It's awful . . . that he doesn't like me enough even to teach me again next year—if he stayed on."

Mary Tucker had often wished for a fourth child who would have been a daughter, but there had been no more after that first three, helter-skelter on each other's heels. She saw that Sylvie was struggling with a girl's thoughts— thoughts that had been sharpened or clouded, as the case might be, with the knowledge that came unasked in the close living of the fettlers' camp. Sylvie knew all about life without yet having lived it. Knew all about life, without knowing herself.

"Is he a nice fellow . . . this Clive Scott?" Mary asked.

"Yes," said Sylvie simply. "He reads to us, Mrs. Tucker—and he took us on excursions in the beginning—only the other kids didn't like them. So we stopped going. I asked him . . . the other night . . . if he would walk with me over the paddocks to see what the min-min was—but he told me to go to bed."

There was the disappointment of a child in Sylvie's voice, but Mrs. Tucker knew that the thing that was hurting her was not altogether a child's emotion. The older woman moved closer to her on the bed and put an arm about her.

"Have you told your mother?" she asked.

Sylvie looked startled. "Oh, no," she said.

"Why not?"

Sylvie smoothed down the skirt of the short dress over her thighs. "She's . . . she's not very well."

"I don't think I've met your mother," Mary Tucker said. "I've met some of the women from that siding, but not your mother. Tell me what she looks like—maybe I'll remember her."

Sylvie looked into Mary Tucker's dark eyes, almost with suspicion, but there was nothing there to frighten her. She thought before answering. There was something she wanted Mrs. Tucker to know. "I love Mum," she told her simply. Then she went on. "She's thin, not like . . ." and she looked away confused.

"Not like me," Mary laughed. "Go on."

"She's very thin—bony—but I don't think she was always like that. No—I'm sure she wasn't." Enthusiasm crept into the young voice. "I saw a colored picture of her once in her wedding dress—just on her own—Dad not in it. It was in a trunk that she doesn't open very often—and I just happened to go into her room when she was looking at it, and she showed me."

The surprise that Sylvie had felt then, at being invited to look at the photograph, was in her voice now. It revealed a deep gulf somewhere in this family relationship. A gulf almost incomprehensible to Mary, whose family was woven close like a dilly bag.

"She was pretty . . . brown hair and brown eyes . . . sort of soft. Course I know photos often make people look better than they are—but I reckon she might really have been like that once. Ruby's like her—and she's pretty. But Mum's had five children—six when the next one arrives—so I reckon that's enough to make a woman stop being pretty. That and living on the siding for so long, so far from everything—and having to leave Sydney."

"Living on the siding for so long and having to leave Sydney would be the real reasons, Sylvie," Mary said.

"I don't want to live on the siding always!" Sylvie told her desperately. "But I don't know how to get out—if Mr. Scott won't teach me! He said I ought to go to the Port to high school—that I'm too old for his school. But it's no good going to high school, if I don't know enough to keep up with the others. George Timms only stood high school for three months—because he was too far behind."

Mary Tucker nodded. She knew what difficulties these outback children—and parents who cared—faced. Many young parents who, like themselves, could not afford boarding school for their children, were driven back to the towns, robbing the outback of a valuable labor force. This would have happened to Chris and her if they hadn't made a special effort, especially as Chris himself had been well educated and believed that his sons should have the same advantage.

Chris had been brought up in the city, but during the Second World War he had been in the army and stationed for some time in the Center. He had fallen in love with the harsh beckoning country, and when the war was over he had returned to stay. But he didn't slough off a love of reading, of books, of acquiring knowledge. These things remained with him. And when his eldest son was old enough, he rented a two-way radio from the government for twenty-four dollars a year, and enrolled each child, in turn, in the School-of-the-Air.

Most days Chris took his tucker-box and was away all day, so that it fell to Mary, as it did to most outback mothers, to supervise the children's schoolwork. But Chris made sure that Mary had the backing of his discipline. School hours were strictly from nine to twelve o'clock in the morning— unless there was a pressing outside job in which he needed Jeff's help—and another hour and a half in the afternoon.

The kitchen, mostly, was the schoolroom. The radio was in here so that Mary could see that her sons kept their minds on their work while she prepared meals, or smoke-ohs, when a team was crutching or tailing in a nearby paddock, or when, three times a week, she went through the day-long cycle of baking bread.

The radio session for each age group was only a quarter of an hour daily, but every fortnight a set quantity of work had to be dispatched to the teacher for marking and correcting. Mary and Chris saw that this was always done and on time. In this way, they kept their children's educational program to a normal schedule and were able to remain in the country they both loved.

But Mary knew there were parents who had had little education themselves and saw no value in it for their children. These children were handicapped from the start. Even where a school and teacher were provided—as at the siding —they couldn't always overcome the difficulty of their environment.

She wasn't surprised when Sylvie said flatly, "In any case, Dad isn't interested in high school. He was only going to give me another year at the siding because I kept at him."

The voice told Mrs. Tucker how difficult it had been to win that concession, now rendered useless.

"Mr. Scott is different from the other teachers we've had," Sylvie went on. "It's easy to learn from him. I like learning now."

Mrs. Tucker guessed that learning had become easier and likable—and necessary to this girl who was growing up— because the teacher was a young man, and earnest.

"That's why—if only he'd teach me next year—I . . . I might get to know enough to do something better than just help in the kitchen at one of the homesteads," Sylvie went on.

"How long have you been thinking all this?"

"Just lately—mostly since Sunday when Mr. Scott told me he was going."

"Clive Scott has a girl, hasn't he?" Mary Tucker asked gently.

"Yes. Down at Whyalla. He goes . . . often . . . to see her."

Mary Tucker was thankful for that answer. At least Sylvie didn't understand or estimate her own emotions. Or did she?

"She's thin—like me. But she has nice hair—very bright and golden. But she spoils it by pulling it tight back into a bun. She's not really pretty."

There was satisfaction in the girl's voice.

From the kitchen the tinkle of knife on fork and the banging of crockery had ceased, and suddenly Mr. Tucker appeared at the bedroom door. "We'll have to notify these kids' parents that they're here safe," he said.

Sylvie jumped up. "Oh, Mr. Tucker . . . please—not yet! I haven't found out about the future yet."

"The future?"

"I'll explain later, Chris." Mary Tucker frowned at her husband. "And you don't have to ring yet, surely."

"They've been gone more than two and a half days," said Chris. "If you were their mother, wouldn't you be out of your mind by now?"

Of course she would. But she wasn't so sure about Sylvie's parents.

He went back to the passage just outside the kitchen, and they heard him wind the handle of the wall phone. This phone connected the out-station with the Homestead. It had been installed to alert them of firings from Woomera. He rang a number of times and he said, "Hello . . . hello . . . hello . . ." a string of times, and they knew no one was answering. He came back at length. "Phone's out of order," he said. "I can't get through. I'll try the radio on our next call-time."

A bit of color came back into Sylvie's cheeks.

Mary patted the girl's hands. "That's not until tomorrow morning now. Being in Woomera country, we're only allowed to transmit and receive during certain times. It's a security measure—to prevent leakage of information. As for the phone, it might take a day or two to find the break. There'll be time to work out the future. In the meantime, you've walked and slept in that dress for nearly three days—I'll find something else for you to put on. I have a dress here that I can make over for you."

She didn't tell Sylvie that she had been planning to give

it to Knobby's Betty, who was often less than decently clad.

Some of the tiredness went out of Sylvie's face. She watched Mary go to the tall wardrobe with the mirror in the center, and take down a cotton dress that had been pushed well to the back. It was yellow with a pale green leaf design across it, and faded.

Mary shook her head. "No, it won't do," she said. "You haven't enough color to wear yellow. I've a better idea."

She pulled open the drawer at the bottom of the wardrobe and while Sylvie stared with absorbed interest at the things a woman keeps in the bottom of her wardrobe drawer, she rummaged in the corners and finally brought forth a loosely wrapped brown paper parcel. She threw off the paper to reveal a piece of blue floral polished cotton.

She held it against Sylvie, under her chin. "This does something for you," she said, not adding that it was the piece she had bought for herself the last time the traveling salesman had come by. She had told him—the cheeky fellow—that it was the sort of gay cotton that a young girl wore; and he—pleasant cheeky fellow—had asked what was she, anyway! So, of course she had bought it. Now she was glad she had.

"We don't know how long the phone will be out of order," she said, "so I'll put the scissors into it right away."

"For me?" Sylvie's eyes were wide.

"Yes."

"You can sew?"

"Yes—I was a dressmaker in Adelaide before I married Chris. And now—here I am—stuck in the back o' beyond, and loving it. Funny how you get to love this country. . . . Now, let's look at you for size. I'll have to draft a pattern—haven't anything that would be near your skinny fit. I was never as thin as you, even as a child."

"I'm . . . not a child," Sylvie said, her eyes eager on the material.

"Well, not exactly," Mary agreed.

Then they went into the kitchen where the boys had left the table and the bench where the washing up was done quite tidy. The tea towels hung across a line near the stove to dry and the dish cloth had been wrung out and left on the side of the dish. But the kitchen was still very full, with five cats in varying shades of marmalade sitting on the hearth and purring in varying keys. The kitchen belonged to the cats as much as to anybody.

Mary gave the table an extra wipe with a dry clean cloth, and spread out the material. Sylvie thought she had never seen anything so beautiful. It shimmered in different shades of blue, as the sea shimmered, as she had seen it shimmer at Port Augusta.

Mary turned it this way and that, working out the details of the style. Then she got out some old newspapers and began to make lines here and there with a piece of red chalk from Peter's pencil case and to take measurements, frowning as she worked. Sylvie stood in the middle of the kitchen, ready to be measured from any angle, frightened to speak lest she break the spell, tiredness, sunburn, blistered feet forgotten.

Mary worked swiftly because this was her old trade and she had been a good, clever dressmaker. Soon the draft was ready and transferred to the cotton. Sylvie watched, with some trembling, as the scissors sliced into the gleaming surface. She couldn't believe that this woman was making a dress for her. No one—as far back as she could remember—had ever made her a dress. Something cheap off the rack in Coles at the Port or, more often, something handed down from someone else. Her mother couldn't sew.

"I should have had a daughter," Mary said. "I love making pretty things—that's why I dress dolls for hospital bazaars and race stalls."

All afternoon Mary cut and tacked and sewed on the old machine that ran swift and delicate and soft as a new one, for Chris kept it oiled and cared for. In the middle of the afternoon Mary told Sylvie to make a cup of tea and get some currant biscuits out of the tin. They sat quietly for a little while and drank their tea, while the cats purred and Sylvie looked at the dress on the table that was already taking shape.

"Mrs. Tucker," she said, "I've never seen a dress *happen* before . . . it's like magic. Your fingers are magic—to be able to make something so beautiful, just out of your head."

"Wait until it's finished, Sylvie, for the compliments," she said, but she was pleased all the same, and she knew by the feel in her fingers and the zest for the sewing that it was going to be a good dress. Neither of them thought of the male creatures who had been around for the midday meal. Sylvie didn't even think of Reg except to suppose, vaguely, that he was outside somewhere with the three boys; and to glance outside and notice, just as vaguely, that the pebbles and twigs and sand were still racing before the fierce wind, but that patches of the sky now were almost black.

In the intimacy of making this frock, she knew that she and Mrs. Tucker should be talking about the future, but somehow it wasn't nearly as important now as the dress. Once she thought about the telephone line and hoped it wouldn't be mended quickly. And she stroked the contented cats, and thought, "When I'm married, I'll have five cats too."

Her father didn't like cats so they had never owned a cat, even at the siding.

# Chapter **Eleven**

MR. TUCKER HAD left the kitchen after trying to make the phone call. "I'll have to get that bike back on the road," he said. "Those rams have to be brought in."

"I'll come and help, Dad," Frank, the middle Tucker, said eagerly.

"You couldn't help at this stage," his father said. "It's one of those delicate little repairs that two pairs of hands could botch."

"Let me do the whole thing—I'll have her running as sweet as a bell."

"Don't doubt you would, boy—but to get her bell-like takes time. All I want is to get her going—quickly. I'll give you a call if you can be of use."

He had gone out then, leaving the boys with the dishes.

Reg didn't like helping with the dishes. At home he always slipped out to Timmsee's when the washing up was imminent. In any case, like his father, he wasn't really expected to help at home. There were Sylvie and Ruby, and now Ann coming on, to whom dishes were a heritage. The domesticated way the Tucker boys wiped out the washing-up dish, and hung up the tea towels to dry, disgusted him. He had dried the plates that came his way—after first explaining that he was likely to drop the cups with their silly handles—as slowly as possible, thereby intimating that he wasn't really a drier of dishes. Some of his cocksureness had returned with this dish washing. The fact that the boys hadn't mentioned the embarrassing subject of the rock hole had restored his confidence. He and Timmsee together would find it exciting to take on these three!

In any case he wasn't particularly anxious to please his hosts. He knew he had made a bad mistake in listening to Sylv—all this talk about getting advice about their future! He knew what his future would be if he kept on letting her run his affairs! Magill Reformatory Institution! He was sure now that they should have run away separately—each would have had a better chance of getting away. He would have, anyway. Now old man Tucker had made it clear that he would send out news of their whereabouts as soon as possible. And with the plane from Woomera in mind he had no intention of facing his father.

As he rubbed the tea towel around and around the plate —until Peter said to leave the pattern—he planned his moves to get away from Gulla Tank. And thinking of Knobby, and the opals in his pocket, he didn't expect it to be too difficult.

When the dishes were finished, Jeff and Frank picked up the two small rifles from the rack by the door and a handful of bullets from a box.

"Are you coming outside, Reg?" Jeff said. "Or have you had enough of the wind and heat?"

Reg might have answered yes to the last question if his interest hadn't been taken by the guns. He had noted the rifles almost as soon as he entered the kitchen.

"We always have an hour or so free after lunch before we do more school work, and we like to get outside—hot or not," Jeff added. "We haven't had much target practice this week. A wind like this makes it more interesting."

Reg nodded and followed the three boys across the stony

ground, past the wood heap, the fowl house, and the air-raid shelter. Once his left hand slid into the pocket of his shorts to make sure that the opals, wrapped in a bit of rag, were still there.

Looking at the boys, it was easy to see that they were brothers, all with the same dark hair, solid build, and straight shoulders. Only the height varied. Jeff would have been as tall as his father even without the high-heeled, elastic-sided boots, but Frank was much shorter. In fact there was not much difference in height between him and Peter.

As they were passing the air-raid shelter, Frank dived in and came out a second later with an old kerosene tin.

"We keep all the rubbish in there," he grinned. "Very useful as a storeroom."

"Do you go in there when there's a firing?" Reg asked.

"Well, we get phone warnings, of course. But it depends on the rocket. Mum doesn't like the Black Knight or the Blue Streak—if either of those is on the program, she sees that we do."

"Pity women can't appreciate rockets," Peter put in sadly. "The Black Knight generally goes up at night—not later than eleven o'clock. So Mum switches the phone across to the air-raid shelter—that's so we can be notified when it's all clear—and musters us down there. Sometimes they fire a Black Knight two nights running—and then not another perhaps for six months. But there're always plenty of Sky-larks—they look good streaking up the sky at night."

"I might tell you," Jeff laughed, "that Mum has to hang on to Peter by his shirt tail to keep him in there."

"Well, I have to learn all about rockets and planes," Peter grumbled, "and I like to see the lights and flames zooming across the sky." His voice brightened. "Sometimes, afterward, we find bits of burnt-out casing out in the mulga, though the recovery officer is pretty smart at locating them."

"Reckon I'd be out in the open—getting a grandstand view," Reg declared.

"Not if our mum was your mum," Peter said. It was the one thing in which his mother disappointed him.

As they walked on, they passed a small fenced paddock with a myall tree in one corner. A well-groomed black horse stood braced against the wind, head down, long tail between his legs.

"A horse?" Reg was surprised.

"What else d'ye think it might be—a camel?" Jeff asked.

"No-o. But I thought only bikes were used on Gulla Homestead."

"Not entirely. They keep a few horses at the Homestead. There are some stony hills and heavy sand country on a couple of the other out-stations—they use the horses for mustering. But Dad bought Bender for us to ride. He says every outback fellow must be able to ride—even if there are stations that don't keep horses any more."

"Have you only got the one?"

"Yes. Can't afford to keep more. We've had to hand feed him ever since we've had him—costs money. Anyway, we don't mind sharing. Later on, if it ever rains—and there's feed about—we might get another."

"Is that why you only have two rifles?"

"No. Peter'll get one—when it's time."

Reg might have asked what he meant, but Frank had already drawn a white circle with chalk on the rusty tin, and placed it on a post on the netting fence, and Jeff was taking aim. He didn't hurry the shot. The wind had increased, and he quietly judged and allowed for the veloc-

ity. Then, eyes squinted down the sights, he pulled the
trigger and the bullet ripped through the wind-dirty air.
It was a good shot, nearly a bull's eye. Reg acknowledged
to himself that only good markmanship could score in such
a wind. Then he saw Jeff open the breech and slip another
cartridge in.

"Isn't it a repeater?" he asked, amazed.

"No."

"What about yours, Frank?"

"No—same kind."

"Gee—that must make you mad—having to reload every
time."

"We'll get a repeater when we're eighteen," Jeff said in
that slow quiet way that made him sound so much older
than he was and irritated Reg because it made him feel
young and so much less knowledgeable. "Dad says, by then,
you're old enough to know how to handle a dangerous
weapon."

Reg gave a sniff. "I know how to handle a dangerous
weapon now. Give me a go with that thing."

Jeff looked him over. "How old are you?"

"What's that got to do with it?"

"That's a rule Dad made—you can't handle a gun until
you're twelve."

"Course I'm twelve," lied Reg. "Give it to me."

With some uncertainty Jeff handed over the gun. Although it was a single shot it was a beautifully made little
piece. Reg raised the gun, cushioning it well into his shoulder and, resting his cheek on the butt, took aim. It was a
bit wide of Jeff's bull's-eye—he hadn't judged the wind as
well, perhaps because he was tired. He was disappointed.
He knew he could do better than that. He and Timmsee had
practiced a lot behind the school. They'd riddled the gal-

vanized iron sides of the boy's outhouse—until old man Timmsee had hidden the ammunition. "Costs too much for kids to waste," he said.

"Give me another bullet," he said, and held out his hand to Jeff.

With obvious reluctance Jeff passed over another bullet. While Reg reloaded, Frank stepped forward and took his turn. His shot, too, was a near bull's-eye.

Reg felt disgruntled. These one-bullet-at-a-time marksmen were good. But he'd show 'em. He took aim, taking his sights carefully, bracing himself against the wind. The bullet hit closer to the mark but still not as close as the other two boys'.

"What about Peter—isn't he going to have a turn?"

"He's only eleven," Jeff said.

"What of it—yer old man's not about."

Peter kicked a small round stone with sturdy and direct aim toward the tin. "We have to wait until we're twelve," he said. "I've only six months to go."

"Gee—I couldn't wait!" And Reg reached again for Jeff's gun.

This time he topped Jeff's and Frank's best marks.

Just then they heard the engine of the motorcycle start up on the other side of the air-raid shelter. It throbbed with a quick, uneven rhythm.

"Dad's got her going," Peter said.

"Yes—but listen to her!" Frank was frowning. "Missing every second beat!"

"Dad's bringing her over here," Peter said.

The bike was certainly on the move, though slowly. As it rounded the air-raid shelter, they saw Dixie—a lithe brown shape—come racing after it. Afraid that her master was setting out into the paddocks without her, she leaped onto the space between him and the engine, well padded for her comfort, where she always rode. She pressed into the angle of Chris's leg, crouching down, tail curled in, but rump sticking out a little. She was set for any distance, but was just as happy to leap off when Chris braked to a stop. Her amber eyes seemed to laugh as she barked at the boys.

"Not exactly a day for target practice," Chris said.

"Reg is a good shot, Dad," Jeff said. "Got a bull's-eye."

"Oh. . . . Did you ask Reg how old he is before lending him your gun?"

"Yes—he's old enough."

Mr. Tucker looked at Reg with those direct hazel eyes, and the gray foam of eyebrows on the top. "How old are you?"

The boy's own eyes dropped before that steady stare. He twirled a pebble with his bare foot. "Old enough," he muttered.

"Are you twelve?"

Reg felt his face going hot. This man wouldn't accept a lie. "Nearly . . . " he said.

"How near?"

Reg gulped. This old man Tucker was a sticker.

"I was eleven last month."

"I see—younger than Peter. Then you don't handle a gun while you're in my care. That's a Gulla Tank rule. We don't break rules here."

Reg hated having to admit the lie in front of the boys. It took away some of his assurance—made him a little less than they. Oh, anyway—what were they but a lot of squares!

He thrust his hands into his pockets and drew lines and circles in the sand with his big toe.

Mr. Tucker patted the B.S.A. engine. "Got her going,

Frank," he said, "but not like that bell you talked about. Could be a bit of trouble with the timing gear. I think you can help me now if you come back to the shed."

"All right, Dad." Frank was eager.

"Frank will be the best mechanic in South Australia's nor'west when he's been through technical school and served his apprenticeship," Peter boasted to Reg. "He's going to serve his time at the Port, and go to night school—beginning next year. He can fix anything that busts on a motorbike."

"Pete—you'll swell his head," warned Chris.

"Frank's the only one in our house who really believes mustering should be done on a bike," Jeff put in with a slow grin. "Dad uses a bike—because the boss says so—but you like horses best, don't you, Dad?"

"I do that. A horse has an affinity with the soil and the sheep and the cattle. He knows when to wheel—or dig his heels in—when they make a break. A bike doesn't always respond—will up-end you in sand or spin over on stones if you ask too much too quickly. But she moves fast, of course—and that's the thing nowadays. A bike cuts the time of most station jobs by two-thirds. That's money." He turned to Reg, whose eyes were still on the figures drawn by his big toe. "Can you ride a horse?"

"Not properly. I've only been on a few times."

"Then give him a lesson, Jeff. Not that you can really be taught to ride a horse, Reg."

The boy looked up.

"You can be told how to saddle, how to mount, how to hold him—you can be told to ride in stirrups when trotting, or take the weight off his back when cantering—but you have to learn to *ride* yourself."

The boy couldn't hide the interest in his eyes.

"Don't give him a saddle, Jeff. He'll tend to use the stirrups with a saddle—bareback he has to get his balance to sit there. Now, you come with me, Frank—we'll see if we can trace this new trouble with the bike."

At any other time the thought of getting on a horse would have thrilled Reg. He had always wanted to ride. At the Kingoonya Races, he always stayed as near to the horses as he could—willing to feed and water them just for the pleasure of being with them, of grooming the warm soft hides.

But now he was discomfited in front of the boys. What was more, he felt that this discomfit was unreasonable. Why, Timmsee would think these were nothing but silly so-and-sos! And what would Timmsee have said if old man Tucker had bawled *him* out!

Chris turned the B.S.A. and, with Dixie once more in his lap and Frank running behind, headed back toward the repair shed, while Jeff, Reg, and Peter made for the horse paddock.

Bender was no longer standing under the myall tree, tail down, rump taking the brunt of the wind. Instead he was racing around his enclosure, heels raising a red dust screen, black tail zooming out like a flowing rudder. Every now and again he eased his pace just long enough to high-kick his heels.

"Good heavens!" cried Jeff. "What's got into him!"

"Reckon he's excited," Peter said. "Maybe he likes the wind."

"Hasn't liked it any other day; he's usually lazy in the heat."

"Maybe he senses something," Reg volunteered. "A horse bloke told me once that horses sometimes *know* things. . . . "

"Like what?" said Jeff darkly, taking the bridle off the fence post.

Bender's laziness had certainly vanished. The more dust and sweat he raised, the better he liked it.

Jeff whistled to him several times, but he took no notice except to race harder than before. Jeff entered the yard then, bridle in hand, while the rest of the group watched.

Bender was not caught easily and Jeff was out of breath himself by the time he brought the horse to the gate.

"I don't know whether you ought to ride him," he said, worried. "I've never seen him in this excited, flashy mood before."

That was enough for Reg. It was bad enough being proved a liar, but to be branded coward as well within the space of minutes was too much. In any case he was not afraid. He stepped forward.

Jeff held Bender's head while Peter gave Reg a leg up on-to the hot back; then he handed him the reins. "You know how to guide him, do you?—pull on the reins whichever way you want to go?"

"Yes—I know that much."

Jeff was still worried. "You'd better walk him around un-til you get used to being up there—especially as he's ex-cited."

Walk him around!—like a timid girl!—when the very feel of the animal against his bare legs was a joy, and Bender himself had quieted for him to get astride. He gripped the horse with his knees, as he was told, walked the animal a few yards from the gate, and then urged him with a prod and a whisper into a faster gait.

Bender began to trot, to canter, and finally, with a toss of his head, to gallop. Reg soon found he couldn't match the rhythmic motion. He bobbed and bounced, slid forward to Bender's neck, slid back to his rump, slid from side to side. The grip of his knees was not enough to hold him. All the time he was determined not to fall in the red dust with the two boys watching.

Reins and mane became one as he twined the fingers of his hands into them. Soon he was riding high on Bender's neck and sometimes his legs flapped so that he looked like a flag in the wind. But he hung on.

He had never been so jangled in his life. Up and down, back and forth, side to side. Now into the face of the scorching wind—now pursued by it. Around and around, faster and faster. . . .

But he felt the horse's excitement—felt the tingling that had to have outlet. And so he went with him, making no attempt to pull him to a stop. Satisfied to bounce and bound —only determined to stay on his back. Presently his legs stopped flapping and he began to bounce with rhythm.

Jeff was running after them now, shouting to the horse, to the boy on his back.

"Pull him up, you idiot! D'ye want to break your neck! Pull him up! Bender!"

But Bender continued to race. . . . And suddenly there was no more jangling. With great joy Reg realized he was *riding* the horse.

Jeff stopped shouting.

The next time they passed, he sprang at the animal's head. He grabbed the right rein, hung on, slithering, disappearing in the cloud of dust as he was dragged along, and shouted again, "Bender—you fool! Bender—stop it!"

Bender loved his young master and began to ease his pace, but not quickly enough. Jeff's fingers lost their grip on the rein. He fell. For a second the dust and the hoofs and Jeff were one.

Above it all Reg heard Peter yell. "Jeff!"

He felt Bender balk, felt him quiver, then shoot ahead, but only for a few more yards. The horse eased smartly of his own free will.

Reg looked back to see Jeff getting to his feet, shaking himself as a dog might who had been rolled in the dust. Reg turned the horse toward the gate, hearing Peter's anxious query.

"You all right, Jeff?"

At the gate Reg had difficulty in freeing his hands from the reins and mane, while Bender stood quietly, sides heaving.

"Why couldn't you pull him up!" Jeff demanded.

"I didn't try," Reg said honestly.

"You didn't try!"

"I was enjoying it—he was, too."

"Enjoying it! Getting thrown round like a bag of sugar!"

"It was bumpy," Reg admitted, and rubbed a bruised spot. "But he was excited—made me excited, too. Anyway I was just getting the hang of it."

Jeff rubbed the red dust from his butcher's blue shirt. It seemed that he had no comment to make.

"Reg, something flew out of your pocket as you went round," Peter said. "Dropped just near the myall."

"Out of my pocket!" Reg felt the pocket in which he carried the opals. It was empty! Suddenly pale, exhilaration flat, he slid from Bender's back and shot toward the myall tree.

Peter followed him. "What was it?"

"Just something," Reg said over his shoulder. "Where exactly did it land?"

"About here."

Reg dropped to his knees, scrabbling in the red dust.

"Valuable, is it?"

"Yes . . . yes, it is!" Reg scrabbled harder and Peter got down on his knees, too.

"Here's something!" Peter cried. "Something wrapped up in a bit of rag. Would this be it?"

And before Reg could turn and spring to his feet, Peter had torn off the wrapping. In his hand lay the two pieces of opal.

"Opals!"

"What d'ye have to do that for!" Reg shouted. "They're mine! You didn't have to take the rag off!"

Chin thrust forward, eyes threatening, he grabbed back the two stones.

Peter's eyes blazed, too. "Take it easy!" he warned.

Just then Mr. Tucker, Frank, and Jeff arrived under the myall tree. Chris and Frank had heard the shouts and the thudding hoofs from the repair shed, while Jeff had only waited long enough to hitch Bender to a post before joining in the search.

"What's going on here?" Mr. Tucker demanded.

Peter turned away. It wasn't for him to answer.

"I lost something—but I've found it again."

"What was it?" Once again that inexorable directness that demanded an answer, and Reg knew that there was nothing to be gained—not even time—by holding back. He opened the palm of his hand to disclose the two pieces of opal.

"Opals!" Mr. Tucker took them from the boy and looked at them. "M-m-m, very good opals. Where'd you get them?"

"From a bloke."

"What bloke?"

"How do I know? Only saw him for a few minutes. I

got him a drink of water—he paid me with the opals."

Mr. Tucker looked hard at the boy. He saw by the aggressiveness of ownership that he was telling the truth.

"That's good opal, Reg. Do you think you'd better let me mind it for you?"

"No!" Reg said, and held out his hand.

Mr. Tucker handed the stones back. He didn't know enough yet about the situation regarding this boy and his sister to feel he had any right to insist on minding the opals, so he changed the subject.

"Jeff pulled that horse up just in time. Frank and I heard the commotion and were on our way here—saw what happened. You were heading for a nasty fall."

Reg was silent. He was too dismayed at the disclosure of his treasure—and to old man Tucker of all people!—to think about what had just happened on the horse.

"Jeff could have been injured—he took a risk," Mr. Tucker pointed out sternly.

"Not a real risk, Dad," Jeff said. "Bender's not a bad horse—not disobedient—he was just excited. He began to pull up as soon as he knew it was me at his head. It was my own fault that I slipped."

"Bender's a good fellow," Chris agreed. "In fact, there are no bad horses. If a horse is an outlaw, it's because he's afraid. But if a horse has always been treated well, he behaves well. Fear is the cause of his bad behavior—that goes for humans, too." And Mr. Tucker looked straight at Reg.

Reg put the opals back in his pocket and said nothing. To himself he said pooh-pooh. He'd never been afraid of anything.

In that second the wind blew through them with a great roar, rocking each one on his feet.

"If that gust didn't hit fifty miles an hour, I'm no judge

of wind!" shouted Mr. Tucker. "I think this is excuse enough to ask Mum for smoke-oh."

"I'll give Bender a quick rubdown first," Jeff shouted back.

"We'll wait for you, son—in case you get blown over the fence."

While they waited for Jeff to brush the sweat off the black horse, it suddenly occurred to Reg that Mr. Tucker might have been very angry indeed if he had known that he had made no attempt to stop Bender, or that, if he had, Jeff wouldn't have been nearly trampled on. The two boys could have told him, of course, but they hadn't done so. Reg felt something like warmth in his heart as he looked at Jeff and Peter.

# Chapter **Twelve**

ALTHOUGH VERY UPSET about the disclosure of the opals, Reg was not completely miserable as he watched Jeff give Bender that quick but thorough rubdown. There was satisfaction in knowing that he had stayed on the horse's back. He had been afraid when he mounted—not of the horse, but of the possibility of making a fool of himself in front of these fellows who knew about horses. When you looked a fool, you were out of step, out of line, and that made a bloke feel low, took away his confidence.

He couldn't resist giving Bender a friendly slap on the rump as Jeff turned him loose, and grinned as the horse shot away, excited as before, tail streaming, giving snorting shakes of his head, and opening his nostrils wide to sniff the air.

"He's mad." Jeff shook his head. "All that energy in this heat!"

The group turned then toward the house, breasting the wind that, since that mighty gust, had increased to such velocity that they had to fight to make headway. Above, one half of the sky was a heavy black, the other still blue, the sun strong. The air was dirty with scraps of dead leaf, twigs, pebbles, and was dry as the earth itself.

Reg was glad when Jeff opened the cane-grass gate, and they pushed up the red path between the jade lawn and the rainbow beds, where flower heads were bending low, many of them snapped off. He was dry himself, and edgy every time Mr. Tucker looked at him, which was often. He knew he must be wary of Mr. Tucker. He was the kind of man who knew everything.

Just as they stepped onto the veranda lightning lit their faces. Immediately the sky banged with thunder, and the next moment it started to rain big, splashing drops. The skin of the cloud burst and the water hit the iron roof like a hammer on a drum. Down it spilled in a great pouring of water, as though someone were emptying giant buckets over the house.

Mrs. Tucker and Sylvie came running from the kitchen. Mrs. Tucker had a piece of the blue material in her hand and pins in her mouth. She grabbed the pins quickly, to let the words tumble forth. "A rain!"

"A rain!" echoed Mr. Tucker.

"A rain!"

"A rain!"

The words ran and jumped and splattered from one end of the enclosed veranda to the other, as the Tuckers and Sylvie and Reg ran back and forth to get a better view.

And then they realized a strange thing. Forty yards beyond the front of the house it was not raining! They were looking through a curtain of water to where the desert was still dry, where the wind was still driving the sand and the sticks and the pebbles and the dead leaves ahead of it. The defenseless earth was being whipped and goaded and dessicated into fine red particles, and driven before this burning breath. But behind the house the black cloud stretched to the horizon and it was raining all the way.

"I've never seen rain like this!" Sylvie cried and her face was alight and alive. "I'd like to walk in it!"

"And I want to smell it—up close!" Mary Tucker said, excited. "So we'll both walk in it!"

There were a couple of sacks lying on a stool behind them, and she caught them up.

"Put this across your shoulders, Sylvie," she said, and holding the ends of her own bag under her chin, she opened the wire door and stepped out into the rain.

"After two years! There's no smell like it in all the world!" she cried, and she sniffed the warm greedy smell of the earth as it sucked in the rain, while the boys and Mr. Tucker watched and laughed.

But the woman and girl were soon glad to return to the veranda for even a heavy sack couldn't keep out that kind of wet.

"Hope they're getting it back at the Homestead," Mr. Tucker shouted above the hammers on the roof. "Make the boss happy."

"Now we know why old Bender was excited!" Reg cried. "He knew the rain was coming. He could smell it."

Beyond the curtain of water they could see the stretch of blue sky and the hot sun still shining.

"It's a strange sight," Mr. Tucker said, "and if the rain doesn't spread farther than that edge, you'll be able to see, in a few days, a green belt and a stretch of desert side by side."

They watched silently then, awed by the continuous pouring of the water. Then they began to see other things, too. Bush creatures were coming from the line of mulga, some flying, some hopping, some finding it hard to make the distance because the heat had exhausted them and the crosswind was so strong.

Reg and Sylvie had not seen many birds as they had come along the track, but now there were hundreds of galahs leaving the mulga and struggling toward the wall of water; there were crows and crested pigeons and ground plovers, finches and mulga parrots and several wedge-tail eagles. The birds were taking no notice of each other, even those who were generally enemies. They wanted only the water and the coolness.

Those who reached it were satisfied to have the rain wash over them. The eagles lay with wings spread, taking no notice of the lesser birds, and the lesser birds took no notice of the eagles, while the black-coated crows moved sedately, politely, among the other feathered creatures.

But the cross-wind made the distance almost too far. It buffeted them, tossed them around the sky, tried to turn them aside from relief and drink. Sometimes they fluttered to the hot earth to rest against the onslaught.

The humans on the veranda watched their struggles. Several of the galahs were down and they waited eagerly for them to rise and struggle on. But time passed and they stayed there on the hot stones, their feathers fluffed, their beaks open.

Suddenly Reg shot from the veranda. He ran through the rain and into the dust storm and across the pebbly ground to where the first of the birds lay. The galah tried to rise as he approached but flopped again. Reg picked it up and ran on to the next. This one made no attempt to rise. With a bird in each hand he hurried back to the curtain of water. Once within its coolness he let the bundle of pink and gray feathers and gasping beak flutter to the wet earth.

Sylvie looked at Mrs. Tucker. "He's always kind to animals," she said. "He's not really a bad boy."

Then out of the dust storm came an old man kangaroo and his doe, followed by a young joey. Less than a quarter of a mile from the house they entered the rain curtain. And here for a time they stopped to rest. They took no notice of the house, or the humans who stood at the open fly-wire door.

Reg looked at Mr. Tucker, an anxious query in his eyes.

"I don't kick a man when he's down, Reg," Mr. Tucker said. "Why should I shoot a kangaroo? In their extremity they've hushed their fear—in fact, they know there's nothing here to be afraid of."

In the next short while, the boys made a number of further rescues, then they noticed that the blue partition was going from the sky.

"The rain's spreading," Mr. Tucker said. "See—it isn't a curtain any more. It's stretching to the horizon. I'll go and take a look at the rain gauge."

He came back at a run, gleeful.

"One hundred points already—that's a rain! Of course, we don't know how far it extends, or whether we've just had a cloudburst here. If that phone was in working order, it would be running hot with news now." His face sobered. "This kind of rain brings down fences—creates washaways —makes roads impassable. I hope no emergency arises." He looked hard at Reg again. "We're dangerously isolated when we've neither phone nor road."

And Reg rubbed his cheek hard, as though it were itchy, so they would think that was the reason for the dull red color that suddenly flushed his face.

# ॐ
# Chapter **Thirteen**

SYLVIE WAS GLAD when Mrs. Tucker got over the excitement of the rain, picked up the piece of blue material and the pins, and went back into the kitchen. The rain was a very wonderful experience—the kind of experience she would like to have discussed with Mr. Scott, savoring the detail with him—but the dress was even a greater experience. Nothing must prevent the finishing of the dress—and there wasn't much time. Sooner or later the telephone wire would be mended and the tracks dried out—and then the future would be upon them. But if the dress were finished it would take the edge off the other things that would happen.

She was glad that the four boys stayed on the veranda. Reg wouldn't be pleased with the dress—he wouldn't understand how wonderful it was. He would think that she was being led aside by this frippery—that she was forgetting the deadly seriousness of his plight. She didn't want him to think that, she didn't want to hurt him by giving him the impression that she was more concerned about her own affairs.

She heard Jeff say, "What about a game of quoits?" and Reg's eager reply, "Got quoits, have yer?"

And then quickly came the thud of the hemp disks on the stone veranda and the shouts of the boys as they played.

Sylvie sat down at the big kitchen table, chin resting on

hands supported by knobby elbows, to watch Mrs. Tucker fit the pieces together.

"I think you could help me with some tacking, Sylvie," Mrs. Tucker said. "Might speed up the job. Look—take these pieces of the skirt. I've pinned them, but this polished cotton is better tacked as it's inclined to slip. Hold it very carefully and make sure the edges are even."

Sylvie threaded her needle and took hold of the shining pieces of material. She had never sewn new material before. The only sewing she had done was to put buttons on the children's clothes, darn socks, let down hems and, of late, put patches on Reg's and Billie's trousers. They didn't own a machine, and she had never used one.

The temperature had dropped rapidly, and it was pleasant in the kitchen now, even though there was enough fire in the stove to keep the big pot of mutton stew simmering for the evening meal. The lighting was poor, for the clouds and the rain dimmed the daylight. But because it was still day and the free-lite was for the darkening, she squinted to thread the needle, and Mrs. Tucker moved the sewing machine nearer the open doorway.

Then Mr. Tucker came in and stood on the hearth, disturbing one of the cats who sprang from chair to dresser shelf, and onto the top of the dresser itself, where it sat glowering at the gray-haired man.

With a slow but rhythmical massage of the rear of his overalls with tough-skinned hands, Mr. Tucker collected his thoughts. Sylvie realized that he was about to say something, and she sat doing her tacking with an empty feeling in her middle.

"We'll have to get you back home, or into the Homestead," he said, "just as soon as possible."

Mary looked up from the whirring machine.

"There's no hurry, Chris," she said. "No one will expect you to rush through the wet—everyone will understand that it's raining."

"Would you understand—if you were worrying about Jeff, Frank, and Peter?"

"No," said Mary, but was obviously comfortable in the fact that there never would be such a situation.

"In any case, it's probably unlawful to harbor runaways. I haven't harbored any before, but I haven't any doubt about that. You are runaways, aren't you, Sylvie?"

"I . . . I don't know," Sylvie said. "Reg doesn't want to go back until things are straightened out—but I think I know we'll have to, sometime."

"What did you do to the telephone wires, Sylvie?"

Sylvie looked up quickly, face a little strained. "We didn't do anything, Mr. Tucker."

"M-m-mmm . . ." Mr. Tucker rubbed the seat of his pants more slowly. "Anyway, if I keep you here, without notifying anyone that you're found—and safe—I'll be in trouble with the police, with the Woomera people who sent out the plane, with my boss. No, Sylvie—we'll have to get you back as soon as possible."

"It's going to be hard for Reg," Sylvie said.

"Why especially for Reg?"

"The coppers said last time he was in trouble that he'd be put in some kind of training school next time."

"Reg is a scamp, is he, Sylvie?"

"No. He does things sometimes—things he shouldn't. But he's a good boy inside."

Sylvie loved Reg. He was her brother. She didn't know why he had to do these things that got him into so much trouble.

"A reformatory school might be good for him, Sylvie," Mr. Tucker said.

"It wouldn't be. He'd be too unhappy—he'd do worse things."

"But, don't you see, if your father can't keep him in order —and a training school, you say, isn't the answer, either— what is to be done with him? He, or both of you, just can't run away and manage on your own."

"I don't know what to do." Sylvie looked at Mr. Tucker with eyes that saw no path ahead except that which led to nowhere. She *knew* it led to nowhere. But there were so many people, like the coppers, even like Mr. Tucker at this moment, who couldn't see what she saw. She looked across to Mrs. Tucker, and the woman smiled at her.

"Sylvie came to us to talk about these things," she said, "to talk about the future. It can't all be said at once. Give the kids time. I've never known you so impatient to make a move."

"And I've never known you so careless of another mother's feelings," said Mr. Tucker tartly. "And what about my job, and the officials at Woomera, and the police? You'll have me in jail if you don't watch out."

He shifted a bit sideways so that another marmalade cat complained as he caught the tip of her tail. It, too, sprang from hearth to chair, from chair to dresser, and from dresser shelf to the top of the cupboard, so that there were two cats glowering balefully down on Mr. Tucker, who had usurped their position on the hearth.

There was a frown above Mr. Tucker's hazel eyes. He felt that Mary was being most unrealistic about the whole situation. But then, perhaps a woman who could tie back her dark curls with a red ribbon when she had a son as big as Jeff was unrealistic about some things.

The fire was warm on his back but he didn't move away from it. The hearth belonged to him, not to the cats.

Sylvie pushed her piece of sewing toward Mrs. Tucker. "I've finished the tacking," she said.

The woman looked at it carefully. "You've done it very well, Sylvie. Neat as a pin."

The girl smiled and her face became alive, but the eyes filled with worry again when she looked back at Mr. Tucker and saw that he still frowned.

"Your surname is Edwards, isn't it? What's your father's Christian name?"

"Joe."

"Joe . . . Joe Edwards. . . ." Mr. Tucker rubbed his chin. "I remember, there was a Joe Edwards in the army—stationed at Alice during the war. A dark-haired, blue-eyed whipcord of a man—ready for anything. I wonder. . . ." He looked at Sylvie. "Was your father in the army during the war?"

"I don't know," said Sylvie. "He's never said."

"I knew this Joe Edwards well—he wasn't married—not then, anyway. What was your father before he became a fettler?"

"I don't know." Sylvie answered between closed lips, because she knew that she should know. She was sure that most children knew something of their father's background. But she only knew the past as far back as she herself could remember, and those were the years on the siding.

"Mightn't be the same bloke," Mr. Tucker said. "The name's not that uncommon."

For some reason or other, Sylvie hoped desperately that he was the same man.

"I'll go and put petrol in Herbie—that's the car, Sylvie,"

Mr. Tucker said, "and make an attempt to get through with you."

"But it's raining as hard as ever," Mary objected.

"Now that it's started, it might rain for days. We could end up by being marooned for a week—harboring runaways. No, I have to try and get them through now, before dark."

"Then we'll all go," said Mary decisively.

"You can come as far as the Dead Dog washaway," said her husband cheerfully. "I might need a push through that bog-hole—then you and the boys can come home and keep the fire burning."

Chris went out, and Sylvie looked at Mrs. Tucker. "I don't want to go yet, Mrs. Tucker," she said. "I want you to tell me what's the best to do now that Mr. Scott won't teach me next year. I'm too old, too far behind, to go to the Port high school. Even if Dad agreed—and that's not likely—the kids'd laugh at me there. I couldn't stand it—George Timms couldn't stand it."

Mrs. Tucker put her arm around the girl's shoulders. "Don't worry, Sylvie—we mightn't be able to solve what's going to happen next year right away. We might have to talk it over with your parents first."

"They wouldn't know," Sylvie said.

"Anyway, don't worry, child. I'll do my best to help you. We'll work out something. I haven't any daughters, but I think I remember what it feels like to be a girl, growing up."

"Is it . . . is it looking for something?" Sylvie asked. "I keep thinking there's something I have to know, something I have to find out. Of course, I know all about babies and things like that—Mum has had so many. But there must be something else—like going after that min-min . . . and finding out what it is. I do wish Mr. Scott had gone with me that night—I felt I could have found out what it is. We'd

have talked about it and . . . and he would have explained
it, like he does the books. And if he didn't know what it
was, he'd have read books to find out."

"P'raps it's just making something of our lives, Sylvie—
p'raps that's what it is."

"I don't know. But if I can find out what I'm going to do
next year—now that Mr. Scott won't have me on his hands—
I think that'll help. Did you find what you were looking for,
Mrs. Tucker, when you were growing up?"

Mary Tucker looked contentedly around her very full
kitchen. "Yes," she said, "I found what I was looking for—
what I wanted. Now, let's get on with this sewing until
Chris gives a shout."

## Chapter **Fourteen**

THERE WAS NO need for Chris to give a shout when Herbie was ready. The big old Ford—bought cheaply because it was such a thirsty vehicle—announced its own arrival at the gate in the cane-grass fence with a blast from its open exhaust. Frank had fitted the open exhaust a couple of years ago. At the time his father had said he doubted he could do it—that he didn't know enough yet about mechanics. But Frank had performed the operation without difficulty. So, although Mary felt the noise was unbecoming and embarrassing to respectable middle-aged people, Chris said that, as Frank had proved him wrong, the Ford could keep its open exhaust. It gave off a blast like the tapping-off of the blast furnace at Whyalla, and the three boys and Chris loved the sound of it. But Mary sat up very straight in the front seat and pretended she didn't even hear it. When she drove into the Homestead alone, she wished it didn't announce her arrival so loudly.

Neither she nor Sylvie put their sewing down until they heard Herbie at the gate. Sylvie looked at Mrs. Tucker sadly.

"There's not going to be time to finish it," she said.

"It'll be finished—if not today, then later."

"What about my knapsack?"

"Better get it. It pays sometimes to cater to a man."

Sylvie didn't know what Mary Tucker meant by that, but she picked up the knapsack from the dresser. It wasn't heavy now. The food was eaten and it contained only the one change of underclothes they had brought, their extra cardigans, the mulga-wood kangaroo, and Reg's boots. Sylvie was wearing Mrs. Hedges' shoes.

Sylvie put her arms through the knapsack loops—it was easier to carry that way—and pulled at the short skirt that it dragged up.

"Grown a bit tall lately, have you?" Mrs. Tucker smiled. "Yes."

Outside, Chris was honking the deep commanding horn.

"All men get impatient when they're feeling self-righteous, Sylvie," Mrs. Tucker said. "That's when you just go along— and bide your time."

Though the sky was a heavy gray-black blanket from rim to rim, it was not raining as they walked down the red path, past the now brilliant jade and the sparkle of the washed rainbow, and through the cane-grass gate. The boys were already in the back seat. Sylvie glanced at Reg as Mrs. Tucker motioned her to get in first into the front seat. His mouth was set, his eyes hard as he looked at her. This was not the boy who had been playing quoits a few minutes ago. This was the wary young tough who did not trust grownups.

Mrs. Tucker climbed in beside her and the big car roared off onto the track, which followed the line of telephone posts from the house.

They started to skid from the start. It was hard to get a firm grip on these red mulga flats when wet. The fowls flew squawking from the wheels that threw the red mud far, and in the back the three Tucker boys laughed uproariously.

It was such a long time since they had seen wet earth or mud.

Half a mile beyond the house the track was a well-worn groove through the mulga. It was only the width of wheel tracks and the sides were a foot deep in places, while between these banks a ribbon of yellow-red water was already lying. Chris opened the throttle and sent the car into it.

"Good firm bottom . . . this bit of track!" he shouted above the engine's roar. "We won't stick!"

"Not here anyway," Mary shouted back. "We should get at least three-quarters of a mile from home."

"This car'll go through anything!" declared Chris. "We'll make the Homestead!"

Sylvie hated his assurance and huddled between them, miserable, afraid of what lay ahead. The car swung from side to side, almost scraping the bank, shooting the yellow water out in a fountain on either side.

Then the narrow belt of mulga thinned and the banks of the track dropped away to a level surface. But it was still as contorted as the tortured pipe line they had followed yesterday. Everywhere a weak spot—a crab-hole—had appeared in the track, vehicles had had to go around, adding another bulge and much to the distance. However, its course was plain enough, with pools—depth unknown—filling every declivity. Either side of the track the gibbers were clean, colorful, and shining. Between the stones the red earth was washed smooth and shining, too.

But despite this inviting smoothness on either side, Mr. Tucker kept his old car bounding and shaking and struggling along the defined course.

"You never get off a track," he told Sylvie. "You might only go a hundred yards out there and strike a crab-hole—

and down you go. And there you're stuck until you get a
Land Rover to pull you out. They're treacherous—these
mulga flats."

"The track is often treacherous, too, Sylvie," Mrs. Tucker
said encouragingly. "It's just two years ago—during the last
rain—that we were bogged at Dead Dog. But of course
Chris has forgotten—it's so long ago."

"You've forgotten that I found a better track through
that bad patch," Chris said. "We won't get bogged today."

"Well, there it is," said Mary, "right in front of you—
and enough nice yellow water to gladden any nor'west
sheep-man's heart."

Ahead lay a slight depression in the flat surface, and
while the track itself was a flood, on either side the water
was only lying in pools.

"It's just as I expected," said Chris with satisfaction. "The
water is lying on the track—that means the bottom is solid
and will take us; on either side, it's mostly disappeared
already underneath—that means plenty of crab-holes. Now
. . . here goes."

The old Ford hit the stretch of water at a gallop. Sylvie
pressed down hard on her seat, and in the back the boys
tumbled with the rolling motion. The car shot from left to
right, almost colliding with one telephone pole and slithering on to the next. The track was following the mulga poles
very closely now.

Every now and again the big car slowed almost to a stop
as the mud and water in the holes sucked at the wheels.
Then Frank would shout, "We're losing traction, Dad—
give it to her!"

And Chris would give it to "her"—who answered to the
name of Herbie. With a great bass growl the car would

lumber up out of the hole and on to the next. If Chris did not get his foot off the accelerator quickly, they would fairly hurtle into the next pool. And so the car slipped and slid and groaned and finally jumped into a hole and stayed there.

"She's losing traction!" shouted Frank. "Give her the works, Dad!"

"She's lost traction, my boy," said his father. "We're stuck."

"I knew we would," said Mary.

"I was afraid we would," said Chris. "That was why I was quite willing for all of you to come this far. Now you'll be useful in getting us out. Take your boots and socks off and roll up your pants, boys."

Mrs. Tucker was about to take off her shoes when Chris said. "You needn't get out, Mary. You take the wheel—that is, when we're ready to give her a go. Now, first thing we need is the spade."

Jeff already had the spade out of the car, and was making a gutter to run the water off the track. With an opening made in the side of the pool and graded away from the track the water ran eagerly, fanning out until suddenly it found its crab-hole and with a gurgling sound began to disappear into the bowels of the earth.

"See what I mean by a crab-hole?" Chris said. "Get your wheels into one of those and you're really in trouble. Now, while the water's draining from this part of the track, the rest of you gather up the gibbers. As soon as we can, we'll get the jack under that wheel and, as we raise it, pack up with stones."

While Mrs. Tucker sat behind the wheel, waiting for the order to start the engine, the rest worked with the spade or gathered armfuls of the wet stones, and Chris, in rubber kneeboots, sought to get a jack under the wheel. If Sylvie hadn't been so thoroughly miserable, she would have seen how funny he looked as, with his hands, he lifted each boot out of the squelch before he could put it forward. Once he stepped right out of the boot and put sock, foot, and the end of his long old-fashioned underpants into the yellow-red mud.

Sylvie gathered stones as quickly and as willingly as the Tucker boys. Not that she wanted the car to get out of the bog, but because it was the least she could do. From the corner of her eye she watched Reg. He picked up stones and he brought them to Mr. Tucker, but he worked slowly. He was looking very sullen, not talking to anyone. Only twice he spoke. The first time was when he lifted a large fat gibber and there underneath were coiled a hundred red legs, eight inches of yellow body, and two inch-long green feelers.

Sylvie was passing with some stones. "Look . . ." he said, his eyes excited. "Pretty, isn't it?"

Sylvie didn't like centipedes but she nodded at him, and noticed that he carefully replaced that stone on the hundred red legs, the yellow body, and the green feelers, and sought another.

Then Mr. Tucker announced that they were ready to get out of the bog.

"Start her up, Mum," he said, "and when I say 'go!'—give her all she's got. The rest of us will push from behind."

Mrs. Tucker turned on the ignition, and the big engine kicked into throbbing powerful life.

In the rear, Chris, Sylvie, Jeff, Peter, and Reg found a convenient spot for their hands, while Frank sought a strategic position on the side close to the driver. Chris shouted, "All ready? Then give it to her, Mum!"

They pushed with one grand united effort. The wheels

spun, the gibbers flew out, the water showered them, and the jack fell over—but the back wheel did not leave the bog. Instead it carved itself a deeper hole.

"Can't understand it," muttered Chris. "She should have pulled out of that. We'll have another try."

They drained more water off, they gathered more gibbers, they jacked up the wheel again, Chris put the other leg of his old-fashioned underpants into the mud, then they pushed again. And when it was over, the back axle was embedded in the mud and the wheel was deeper than ever.

"I told you," said Mary. "There are times, you know, Chris, when you should listen to your wife. Now the car has to stay here until the Land Rover comes out from the Homestead— and we've nearly a mile to walk home in the mud."

"Can't understand it," said Chris. "If you weren't a good driver, Mother, I'd blame you."

"Let's start walking," said Mary.

Frank and Chris helped Mrs. Tucker over the churned-up mud, and they started off.

"Can't understand it," Mr. Tucker reiterated, shaking his head. "We should have pulled out of that. Well. . . ." He shrugged his shoulders and smiled at Sylvie. "At least I did my best to get you to the Homestead, girl. No one can accuse me now of deliberately harboring runaways."

"Yes, you did your best, Chris," Mrs. Tucker agreed. "No man can do more."

Sylvie felt it was indeed a very welcome reprieve, and she knew Reg thought the same. She could see by the jaunty set of his shoulders that the load had been lightened. He went ahead cheerfully with the boys, and Sylvie hoped he had no foolish plans in mind.

It was just as she and Mrs. Tucker neared the veranda that Mrs. Tucker called to her second son. "Frank—get an armful of wood from the wood heap, will you, please? I think the kitchen box is nearly empty."

There was a grin on Frank's face as he dropped back that surely had nothing to do with the job assigned to him. He came close to his mother and said softly, though Sylvie heard, "You know, Mum, we might have got out of that bog-hole if you had taken the brake off." And Frank, a good youth, winked a wicked eye at her.

"Don't take any notice of him, Sylvie," Mary Tucker said. "He thinks because he's going to be a mechanic that he knows everything there is to know about cars and driving." And she hurried ahead, not waiting for any reply Sylvie might make.

Just as they entered the house the rain started again, heavier than before.

## Chapter **Fifteen**

THE GULLA TANK out-station house was small. There were two bedrooms, a sitting room, a kitchen, and a bathroom. The second bedroom was only large enough to take two beds comfortably. Peter and Frank slept in here, and Jeff on the wired-in veranda. There was plenty of room on the veranda. Spare beds were kept out in the air-raid shelter for those city relatives who sometimes paid a visit, and who were generally accommodated on the veranda. But tonight, when the boys carried in the two extra beds, one was put up in the bedroom between Frank's and Peter's beds—for Reg—and the other in the sitting room for Sylvie.

Some of the relief that had been bubbling out of Reg since the crab-hole turned them back went flat when he saw the sleeping arrangements. He had been so certain he would be put on the veranda, where it would be easy enough to tip-toe out the wire door which he knew would never be locked, and so into the night. He would follow the telephone wires back to Knobby's camp and then, with his help, strike directly across to the line. The journey would take only half the time —probably much less—because Knobby's route was half the distance.

Now it would be much more difficult to get out of the bedroom quietly. Nevertheless, he didn't think of abandoning his plan. Anything was worth trying, against what he would have to face when the old man and the police caught up with him. Every now and again he fingered the pieces of opal in his pocket, and thought how lucky he had been to meet that miner from Coober Pedy—and how lucky that Mr. Tucker hadn't insisted on taking care of them.

The night grew cold as the rain continued, and the wind, gentle now, veered to the south. It was excuse enough for the small fire of mulga logs to be lit in the open fireplace in the sitting room.

It was a very pleasant room. The furniture was worn but there was a comfortable chair for each member of the family. The mantelpiece was a shelf of polished mulga wood with many photographs of the boys at different ages, and a vase of artificial pink and red roses at either end. On the back wall was a sideboard with books and china ornaments and two vases of artificial blue delphiniums. The cushions were patterned in a bright pink floral cretonne, cheering to the eye when the desert was brown-red and the mulga leaves dull with dust.

There was always something to do at night in this isolated home. Chris Tucker was a reader and he had taught his sons to be the same. The hours from dark until bedtime were for reading or the current hobby.

Tonight was no different, except that Mary Tucker and Sylvie sewed instead of reading. A book had been put into Reg's hand, and he pretended to turn the pages, but his mind was on the dark stretch of track between Gulla Tank and New Tank. He would have to be careful not to miss each telephone pole in the darkness. He was feeling a bit sick at the bottom of his stomach. It would be better if Sylv were with him, but he knew that she was not going to run any farther. Though what she was going to get from the Tuckers he couldn't imagine.

Sylvie had been given a chair at the side of the fire and

as she stitched carefully under Mary's direction, her face grew hot and her eyes shiny above the flush. She had never felt so much a person before. Even the fact that she knew the Tucker boys were not as relaxed as they would be without her female presence gave her some satisfaction. To cause even a ripple in the life around her was an experience.

Then Chris Tucker said it was bedtime, and soon she was alone in the sitting room with the light out, watching the winking ash of the mulga and wondering what was happening back at the siding. It seemed a long time since they had left. . . .

Was Ruby looking after Ann, or was she sleeping that heavy selfish sleep that would not hear when Ann called? Was her mother's headache better? Would Ruby remember to give her a cup of tea—taking care that the water was properly boiling and no tea leaves swimming on the top of the cup? Sylvie felt a new and unusual worry about her mother. She looked so different from this energetic, rounded, happy Mary Tucker. Why did she have to look the way she did—thin, seldom smiling, no red ribbon in her hair? Why did she have to ask so often to go back to Sydney—and always be given the same answer: no? Sylvie was certain that Mary Tucker would never have to ask or beg many times for anything. And what of her father? How mad was he by now?

She was surprised that she was not afraid of that picture of her angry father. Yet he was much more real to her at this moment than her mother. She knew that if he ever hit her again, it would be for the last time.

For a long time she stared at the quiet rose-pink ash. The glow dimmed and brightened as some intruding breeze whisked over the coals. It was like the min-min, she thought, calling her, mesmerizing her. One night she was going to walk across the paddocks to the min-min. . . .

She didn't know how long she had been asleep when a sharp noise awoke her. It was rather like the clank of metal when a goods pulled up at the siding through the night. But she came from sleep swiftly and knew this was not the clatter of a goods. It was some metal object rolling just outside in the dark passage.

She heard Reg's voice. "Blast!"

Then she heard Chris calling out as he came from the front bedroom, "What's that?"

And Reg answering, "It's me," in an angry frustrated tone. "It's me, Mr. Tucker."

And Mr. Tucker saying mildly, "I thought it might be you, Reg. Sorry about that bucket. I brought it in full of wood chips earlier in the night—and didn't take it out again."

She heard Reg's bitter whisper. "Course yer didn't take it out again—yer wanted me to fall over it!"

Sylvie knew then what Reg had planned. To run away into the night, and try to reach the line. She pressed closer into the pillow and the comfortable bed. How frightened Reg must be that he thought of running off into this desert night alone! How frightened of that reformatory school and the police and his father. And she thought, with vehemence, my children will never be frightened of their father, or me.

She listened to Mr. Tucker talking to Reg. "Go back to bed, boy, and get some sleep. And stop worrying. Perhaps there'll be time tomorrow to take you around some of the waters, and I'll show you how to adjust the mills and work the cocks—maybe some day you'll be able to tend a mill and look after the sheep. I think you would like to work with the animals. Go back to bed, Reg."

She listened for Reg to shout rudely to Mr. Tucker, as he might have done to his father—depending on whether the latter was sober or not. To shout, "I'm not going back to bed!"

But Reg said quietly, "Yes, sir."

Mr. Tucker said, "If you want anything in the night, Reg, just call out—I'll hear you."

Again Reg said, "Yes, sir."

Beneath that quiet tone, Sylvie sensed that Reg knew he was beaten. He could only wait now for that future to catch up with him. Sylvie was suddenly angry. These Tucker boys were not afraid of the future. Why did she and Reg have to be afraid?

It was a long time before she went to sleep again. She listened to the rain beating steadily on the roof. She savored the security and comfort of this bed, and she thought— would it be wrong to wish for this night to go on for- ever?

They awoke to a cool morning with a heavy gray sky, though the rain had ceased temporarily. No mention was made of the bucket.

After breakfast Mr. Tucker said there was urgent work ahead, and he needed Frank's help for the final adjustments to the B.S.A. To everyone's amazement, he decided to let the others off schoolwork, too. The concession, he said, was partly because a study of such a rain and its effects was educational, and partly because the radio was crackling with static—indicating further rough weather in the area—so that it was impossible to send or receive coherent messages.

"We'll take a look at Herbie, too, Mary—to see she hasn't dropped down the crab-hole in the night," he said, as he followed the boys out into the clean, washed morning.

As they disappeared, Mary smiled at Sylvie. "I'll have this dress finished by midday. Now what'll we do about your hair?"

"My hair?" Sylvie repeated.

"You must wash it," said Mary. "I've a lovely shampoo that makes your hair shine." She shook her own dark curls. "It's my one extravagance. I like my hair to shine."

"Mine isn't that kind of hair," said Sylvie flatly.

"I've a few rollers," Mary said, "enough at least to roll up the ends. That's the only part of mine I ever roll. I think your hair would look different if the ends turned up."

Sylvie's face glowed. "Do you think so?"

"Yes. Now try on this dress, and then go and wash your hair."

Sylvie could hardly stand still as the soft smooth dress was slipped over her head, and the full skirt hung gracefully from the waist. How different she looked with the waistline in the right place and the skirt the right length. Still too thin and the face too old, but at least a girl—a growing girl.

"It fits well," Mary said. "I won't have to alter it anywhere."

"I wish I could do this—sew like this," Sylvie said with awe. "Just to think of a dress, and make it."

"Perhaps you will, some day," Mary said. "You sew very neatly. Neatly enough to slip-stitch the hem—after you've washed your hair. Take the big kettle with hot water to the bathroom, and after you've washed well with the shampoo, make sure you rinse your hair properly. Do it several times."

"Yes," Sylvie said. In the bathroom she again took off the short dress and stood in her worn petticoat to wash her hair. Passing the door, Mary saw that she would have to spare Sylvie one of her own few petticoats to wear under the new frock.

When Sylvie came back to the kitchen, her old dress on again and the hair hanging in wet wisps on her shoulders, Mary had the rollers and pins ready. Sylvie sat on a kitchen chair in front of the big stove, two cats at her feet, while Mary rolled the ends to a line with her ears. Mary's hands were roughened with work and not very dexterous for she had had little practice with the rollers, but she was determined that the turn-up would be even.

Once while the hairdressing was in progress, Chris came to the kitchen door.

"If you hear a plane," he called through the wire, "make sure you run out and wave. Make the pilot understand that Sylvie and Reg are here."

"Yes," Mary said. She would have run out without this admonition. She knew that she could not delay the runaways' return without legitimate reason any longer. Neither she nor Sylvie had achieved anything in regard to the future. What could they achieve, anyway? There were indeed the parents, the police, the school teacher, the Woomera officials . . . all these would have a greater say in that future than she or Chris. They had no rights. Sylvie and Reg would be bound by the decisions of these various groups. Mary hoped that it would be a kind decision.

When she had finished rolling Sylvie's hair, she put the dress into her hands. "There is only the slip-stitching of the hem to do," she said. "You can do that while I prepare the midday meal. The boys will come in as hungry as hawks."

Sylvie sat by the table while Mary Tucker made the pastry for a big meat pie for the midday meal. While Mary worked, she gave Sylvie a lesson on how it should be done. Rolled in a certain way, not kneaded more than necessary, and handled sparingly with warm hands. And the meat must be cut up finely, and the onions and the carrots, and a dash of tomato and Worcestershire sauce added to give the gravy a tingle.

Sylvie listened and nodded as she stitched. She had never felt so comfortable in her life. In this over-warm kitchen with the stove-box glowing red, the cats waiting for the scrap pieces of meat and the kettle bubbling, the pull of the rollers on the fine hair of her neck, and the good feel of the dress in her hands.

She felt kinship with this woman whose apron bands disappeared into the crevice at her waist, whose arms, bare from the shoulder, plied the pastry roller so strongly, whose dark curls tightened on her forehead with perspiration as she worked.

Sylvie's hair was pronounced dry and the hem of the dress finished at the same time. When Mary combed out the tight roll around the nape of Sylvie's neck, the hair turned up nicely and evenly all the way round. It would never be colorful hair, but at least it had the shine of a good shampoo and cleanliness.

"You may as well put on the dress and give Chris and the boys a surprise when they come in for lunch," she said.

Sylvie quivered in anticipation. Very carefully the dress was drawn over her head so that the hairdo was not damaged. Then she stood waiting for Mary's comment.

"You look lovely," Mary said. "Go into my bedroom and have a look in the wardrobe mirror. You need a proper pair of shoes, of course—and a pair of stockings."

"Stockings?" Sylvie cried.

"Yes—that dress needs stockings to set it off."

They both went into the bedroom to look in the mirror.

Mary was very satisfied with her work. Never before had she transferred a Cinderella into a princess. Not that Sylvie would ever be beautiful in a glamorous way, but at least this was a very different Sylvie from the girl who had come to her door only yesterday.

Sylvie twisted and turned before the mirror, her lips red with excitement, her eyes and cheeks glowing. She moved her head and shoulders to set the sweeping turn of the hair swaying.

She looked at Mary Tucker. "It's not *me*."

"It is you, the real you."

Suddenly Sylvie stood still and stared at the young girl in the mirror. "I wish Mr. Scott could see *her*," she said. "I think he thought I was awful not to wear shoes."

"You," Mary corrected. "You can always look like that Sylvie—if you try."

Then they heard the boys and Chris come into the kitchen.

"Come and show them!" cried Mary, as excited as the girl herself.

The four boys and Chris stood in a row to look at her. Frank gave a wolf whistle, which made his father frown, but even he opened his eyes wide and exclaimed, "Sylvie!"

Reg just stared for a moment, and then said, "You're grown up—I knew you were sort of grown up, but not like this. Gee—you look nice!"

"You still know how to dressmake, Mum," Chris said admiringly.

"Sylvie did the hem beautifully," Mary said, and Sylvie felt proud.

Mary turned then to busy herself with the pots on the stove, and Chris took up his position on the hearth. She had to go around him constantly as she prepared to serve the dinner, but he had stood in that spot for so many years that she didn't notice.

"We finished the bike, and then—you'll be pleased to know—we got Herbie out of the bog," Chris said, "but we left her there, on hard ground. Didn't want to plow back through that soft stuff."

"It was really very easy," Frank said, and winked again at his mother. "Dad just doesn't know what kept the wheel in that hole."

"You're muddy!" said his mother tartly. "No dinner until you've washed."

Frank went off smiling and whistling.

"I'll be able to get through to the Homestead this afternoon," said Chris, while the cat on the hearth beside him watched the rocking movement of his feet with wary green eyes.

Other eyes looked at him, too, some with fear, some with inquiry.

"I'll go in on my own on the bike," Chris said comfortably. "I wouldn't risk Herbie bogging down a second time. It will be a slippery ride, but I should be back before dark. If it's light enough on the way back, I'll have a look at the Swamp Paddock—I'm worried about those rams in there."

"You wouldn't go on your own yesterday," Mary reminded him.

"I had no excuse to go on my own yesterday—my duty was to return these young people to their parents," Chris said. "I've a legitimate excuse today."

"If you say the right things," Mary said, "Sylvie and Reg might be allowed to stay with us another day."

"I'll try," Chris said simply, and appeared not to notice the gratitude in Reg's eyes.

Because this trip into the Homestead was for an unusual

purpose, and because it so concerned the very lives of Reg and Sylvie, the whole group went out to the gate to see him off.

He was equipped as though he were going for a week. It was one of the rules laid down by the management of Gulla Homestead Station that no stockman rode his bike out from his home without being fully prepared for every emergency. So, as Chris believed that rules were made to be obeyed, the B.S.A. was, as he said, fully armed. He carried a full water bag—despite the rain pools—dry rations, helmet, goggles, a full tank of petrol, and tools. And, as he started up the engine, Dixie came leaping from behind the wood heap to take her place in front of him.

He gave her a welcoming pat. "I'll take her," he said; "she's good company."

Then he opened the throttle, and the big bike leaped away, Dixie's tail escaping from under his arm to wave a goodbye.

"He may or may not be back tonight," Mary said, "depending on those wet tracks. In the meantime, you boys can make an impression on that wood heap, and Sylvie and I will bake some cakes."

Which was Mary's way of saying that they must not sit and worry until Chris returned.

## Chapter **Sixteen**

CHRIS TUCKER RETURNED to Gulla Tank sooner than expected. In fact, he was away only a few hours. The wood heap was much reduced in size and the boys were in the kitchen eating the cakes that Mary and Sylvie had made, when they heard the B.S.A. shut off at the gate. They heard Dixie bark as she leaped from the bike. Her master's sharp rebuke told them that he was either upset or angry:

As he strode into the kitchen, his overalls streaked with the mud of the track, they saw that he was both.

Sylvie, watching anxiously, knew that his mood was connected with herself and Reg.

"You're in time for a cup of tea and a hot cake," said Mary, and took another cup from the dresser. She was relieved when she saw him take up his position on the hearth.

The four boys and Sylvie watched him as he stirred the two heaped teaspoons of sugar into his tea. Chris was never angry without reason, but his boys had found that when he was angry it was best to remain quiet. Mary waited, too.

"I didn't go into the Homestead," he said, as he stirred, "and could have been back sooner. But I stopped to mend a couple of breaks in the fences in the Swamp Paddock. Those rams will have to be moved first thing in the morning —it's boggy."

He planted his feet more firmly on the hearth, his hazel

eyes unsmiling. No one spoke. They were waiting for the reason for his anger.

"When I set out this afternoon, I decided to go by the track that goes past the New Tank," he said; "it's several miles longer but it skirts a particularly boggy patch. I thought it might be the shorter route in the long run. It was." He frowned at Reg. "I found—if I mended the telephone wire—I need not go any farther."

Reg pressed down hard on to the bench behind the table, where he was sitting between Jeff and Peter. The bench squeaked and everyone looked at him. Hot color began to rise from the first visible part of his neck and spread upward slowly and steadily, like an incoming tide, until it disappeared into his dark hair.

"The telephone wire had been cut with a sharp instrument—just outside Knobby's camp," Chris went on. "I found the length of wire coiled on the ground."

And while Reg's face was hot, Sylvie's was pale.

Chris spoke directly to Reg. "Did you know, Reg, that tying the two pieces of wire together again mends the break? I was able—with Knobby holding a ladder of boughs steady—to effect repairs. The telephone is working again."

Reg stared back at Chris, mesmerized.

"I had talked to Knobby—told him you had arrived here safely—before I found the cut wire. At first I blamed him but soon realized he was not the culprit. Then I questioned him. The old man tried hard not to tell me—he wanted to keep faith with you—but I was determined to have the truth. I finally got it out of him that you had asked him to guide you back to the line—the short way—that you would give him a piece of opal if he did."

"A piece of opal!" It was Sylvie's voice.

"Don't you know that Reg has two pieces of opal, Sylvie? Two pieces, I'd say, worth at least two hundred dollars."

"Opals . . . worth two hundred dollars!" Sylvie couldn't believe the words she repeated. She turned to her brother. "Is it true?"

Reg said, in a very low voice, "Yes, Sylv."

"But where did you get them?"

Reg told the story then of the swagman who had asked him for a drink of water, and who paid him with two pieces of opal.

"But why didn't you tell someone! Why didn't you tell *me*!"

"I was going to tell you on the goods, but we weren't together. Then I thought . . . I'd wait . . . and see what happened."

Sylvie blazed. "And the thing that happened—was that you cut the telephone wire! That was what you were doing when you left the wurlie in the night—I remember seeing you come back. Reg—why did you do it?"

But Reg said nothing. He was past explaining why he did things. He wasn't sure himself now why he had cut the wire. Except that at the time it had seemed so important to his chances of getting away to safety. He should have known, of course, that he couldn't get away. Why had he thought he could outwit the grownups who wanted to put him into a reformatory? Why had he been so afraid—yes, that was it, afraid!—that he had cut the wire? His shoulders slumped, his eyes dulled.

"You know how serious this is, Reg?" Mr. Tucker said quietly. "We're very isolated out here. As I said yesterday— with the telephone down and the roads impassable, we're quite cut off. Suppose there had been an accident—suppose

Jeff had been hurt when he jumped at Bender's head yesterday—and we couldn't get him into the Homestead, and we couldn't call for the Flying Doctor?"

Reg didn't look up. There was nothing for him to say.

Bitterness was in Sylvie's eyes as she looked at her brother's lowered head. The comfort of this kitchen was suddenly hers no longer, the pleasure of the lovely dress, the interest of the cooking lesson she had just had, the sharing of this afternoon tea with the three Tucker boys, the marmalade cats, the kinship with Mary Tucker . . . how could he spoil them all in this way?

"You . . . you're worse than I thought you were, Reg," she said, ashamed of him and of herself for the situation they were in.

Reg was eleven. Over the last few days he had carried the burdens of fear and frustration and been the victim of his own misdeeds, misdeeds that he couldn't explain.

But when Sylvie spoke to him like that—and he sensed her hurt and her condemnation, it was more than he could bear. He hid his head in his arms on the table, and though there was no sound of his crying, he couldn't stop the trembling of his shoulders.

Sylvie sat looking at him awkwardly. Reg was not one to cry. Her anger went. She got up from her chair, passed behind the Tucker boys on the stool, and put her hand on Reg's shoulder. "You . . . you didn't mean it, I suppose," she said.

Reg's shoulders still trembled and the kitchen was quiet except for the dropping of a piece of wood in the stove and the purring of the cats. The Tucker boys were silent and embarrassed.

Then Mr. Tucker said, "I'll have to ring the Homestead."

He went into the passage where the phone was on the wall, and they heard him wind the handle, then say "Hello."

They heard his side of the conversation.

"Yes . . . yes, boss—thought you'd be wondering what had happened out here. The line's been down—couldn't get through to you . . . not by road, either. And you couldn't get a jeep out, eh? Yes . . . yes the rain was good. But, listen, boss—I've other news. Do you know if two Edwards children have been reported missing? . . . They have! . . . Then you can tell everyone to stop looking—they're with us. Yes, that's right. With us. Will you notify their parents that they're safe?"

Then there was a lot of talk from the other end before Chris Tucker finally put up the receiver, wound the handle, and came back into the kitchen.

"There's been a search for you," he said, "including the plane. The boss is going to ring through now to Kingoonya—to notify the police that you're safe. They'll tell your parents. He'll ring back here in a few minutes to say what we're to do next."

It seemed such a long few minutes. They sat around the kitchen waiting for the phone to ring. There seemed to be nothing to talk about; even Mary gathered up the cups and saucers and put away the cake tin with scarcely a word. Chris waited on the hearth, frowning. The cutting of the wire seemed to have left him with no further comment to make.

Sylvie watched him, looking for some sign of softening in the stern face. She could only take comfort from the fact that he had not explained what had happened to the line over the phone—he had only said that it was down.

They jumped when the telephone rang, and Mary stopped rattling the dishes so that they could hear what was said.

But this time they gained little from Chris's answers—mainly yes or no. It was a short conversation. Everyone looked at him, even the cats, when he returned to the kitchen.

"They'll send out a Land Rover in the morning," he said; "that is, if it can get through. There's been a tremendous rain between here and the Homestead. Boss said they're still marooned in a lake nearly a mile wide all round."

"So you wouldn't have got through, Chris—if you'd tried to go all the way," Mary said.

"No—I wouldn't have had a chance. But the boss thinks a lot of the water will disappear overnight. So we must be ready. If possible, you'll be taken straight on then, Sylvie, to Kingoonya, where your father will be waiting."

"And the police?" Sylvie said.

"I—I didn't ask, Sylvie—but I would think so."

Reg had raised his head from his arms, but he still sat at the table, very miserable.

Jeff made the first move. "What about a game of quoits?" he said. "Come on, Reg—I'll take you on."

Reg stood up slowly and followed the boys out onto the veranda, while Sylvie turned to dry the dishes for Mary and Chris continued to stand and think and tread near a cat's tail on the hearth.

## ❦

## Chapter **Seventeen**

TO THE SURPRISE of everyone, and the joy of the sheep-men, a great deal more rain fell in the next forty-eight hours. It rained in spasms. Every now and again the sluice gates of the sky opened and poured volumes of water over the greedily sucking earth. It favored some parts more than others. The area between Gulla Tank and Gulla Homestead, particularly around the Homestead, registered the heaviest falls. So that another four days went by before the Land Rover from the Homestead was able to reach Gulla Tank.

These were difficult days for Sylvie and Reg and the Tuckers. Chris soon made it clear that he wanted no further discussion about what had taken place and that normal activities must go on. School-of-the-Air was part of the routine—when the rain stopped long enough and at the right time for reception and transmission without the jumble of static. Reg had to take part in these lessons, just as he was expected to take part in whatever outside work Chris Tucker delegated to his boys. Reg didn't enjoy the lessons because he found that Peter, his own age, was considerably ahead of him. But he did enjoy the outdoor tasks, that is, when he could put the thought of what lay ahead out of his mind.

And there was plenty to do. It began the very next morning, following the mending of the telephone wire. Chris was concerned for the two hundred rams in the Swamp Paddock. They had been brought out from the Homestead to Gulla Tank some months earlier, because the Swamp Paddock contained the best remaining feed in the whole vast area of the Gulla Homestead Station.

Chris roused the family to an early breakfast. "Those rams will have to be got out this morning," he said. "I've been worrying about them all night. Too boggy where they are. I'll move them into the next paddock—there's feed up there already. They can stay there until the boss makes up his mind if he still wants them brought in. I'll need your help on Bender, Jeff. He'll be able to go where the bike would only lie down and spin her wheels. You, too, Reg. I promised to show you something of station work."

They set off immediately after breakfast, Dixie in front of Mr. Tucker, Reg on Bender's back behind Jeff, and Punch loping behind. There had been no rain since midnight, the air was as still as a lizard hoping to be unobserved, and where there was no water lying the red earth had been smoothed to a fine finish.

Bender followed behind the bike. The pace was slow. There was little grip for the wheels and Mr. Tucker had to go around many a sheet of water that Bender walked through.

"Good thing we don't have to ride out far," Jeff said over his shoulder to Reg. "Sometimes a muster is thirty miles out, and if you use horses it means camping out. A thirty-mile ride out to muster—over wet country—is enough for a horse. So you do your mustering the next day. Then there's the ride back. Might be out two or three nights. A bike can do the job in a day." He patted Bender, in case the horse's feelings were hurt. "But I like a horse."

"How far do the rams have to be moved?" Reg asked.

"Only a couple of miles. Quite a high bit of solid country just beyond the fence."

The Swamp Paddock was a large, scrubby mulga flat, but Chris had located the sheep the previous afternoon. He knew they were in a corner close to the swamp, which covered only a small area.

With the motorbike chugging like a motorboat, they wound through the mulga scrub until they came to an expanse of yellow water, dotted with the tall clumps of half-submerged cane-grass, looking like a dwarf water forest. The bike chugged on, but Jeff reined in. To both boys the sight was unaccustomed and wonderful.

"It's years since there's been water in this swamp," Jeff said, "but Dad says it's four or five feet deep in parts and will probably last some weeks."

The edge of the water teemed with life. There were tiny water beetles with red or black heads, tadpoles with inch-long bodies and tails the same length, larger frog-like creatures with a jelly-like overlay of opalescent colorings —blues shot with pinks. These played at somersaulting, spending seconds on their backs, and revealing, almost indecently, their breathing apparatus. There were little fat gray-green frogs, with bulbous black eyes, whose bodies pulsed more on the right side than on the left, hopping and scuttling over the mud or swimming in the water.

"Where does the frog go when the water dries out?" Reg said.

"Where he came from. He burrows farther and farther down in the mud as the sun dries it out," Jeff said. "We've dug him up when we've been digging new post holes— sealed in by dry mud, just waiting for the rain to come again to release him."

Jeff urged Bender forward and they set off after the bike. But they stayed as close to the swamp as possible, neither saying much, both excited by this phenomenon of water in a dry land.

The sheep were still where Chris had seen them yesterday, feeding leisurely on the minute green shoots that were already coloring the red earth. But not all of the mob.

From his extra height on Bender's back Jeff could see that some were already bogged.

"There're about twenty caught on the far side!" Jeff shouted to his father. "You can't take the bike in. Reg and I'll get them out!"

Jeff kicked Bender into a trot, and to Reg's delight he found himself rising and falling as rhythmically as his companion.

Then they came to the trapped sheep.

"This is the best bit of country we've got . . . until it rains," Jeff explained, "but—apart from the swamp itself— it gets water-logged very quickly. They're bogged while they feed before they know it."

There was no way of getting the sheep out except by manhandling them. The two boys slid off Bender's back and Jeff tethered him to a convenient mulga. They stood for a moment to survey their task. Behind the sheep, not far away, the tiny waves of the swamp lapped gently. There were horse-stingers skimming the surface, myriads of butterflies, and the frogs were croaking—some deep and guttural—old-man frogs.

The bogged sheep were twenty animals without hope. The soft clinging clay reached only just above their hoofs, but it held them. They were carrying nearly nine months' wool, and that ten pound fleece had become a thirty pound fleece with the weight of rain. The drop in temperature after the heat, the wet wool, made them cold, stiff, and cramped. With water and feed in sight, they would have stood there until they died of thirst and starvation.

"Are you feeling strong?" Jeff said.

"Yes," said Reg, acutely aware of the other's man-size.

"It'll be just push and heave and drag," Jeff said.

It was indeed push and heave and drag. The suction was like a clamp. Reg watched Jeff tackle the first animal. Each hoof had to be released in turn, then the sheep rolled onto its back, and dragged through the mud on its hindquarters, as a shearer drags a sheep to be shorn from its pen. Once on firm ground the animal lay passive, legs outstretched and stiff, making no attempt to rise.

Having seen how it was done, Reg set to work. At first, that much sheep and wool was almost impossible for him to roll. He rolled himself, several times, once with sheep and wool nearly on top of him, before he succeeded in turning his first sheep. And in the four or five yards to firm ground, he slid or sat down every few feet. But he was tough and wiry, and dug his heels in and strained his muscles.

Jeff didn't give orders or offer advice to do it this way or that. He simply went about the job, taking it for granted that Reg would do his best.

Reg didn't pull nearly as many sheep from the bog as the older boy, but he worked as hard. And while Jeff was muddy to the knees when the last one was freed, Reg was muddy to the eyebrows in front and the top hairs of his head at the back.

A few of the animals made attempts to get up on their legs, but most lay as they were dragged out, their fleeces too heavy for them to lift.

"They're stiff and cold—must get them moving," Jeff

said. "Otherwise they'll die, anyway. When a sheep makes up its mind to die you might as well skin it on the spot."

He began to work the long, woolly legs back and forward, inducing circulation. Again Reg watched first, then followed suit. One by one the rams were coaxed, prodded, or lifted to their feet.

Reg worked on one animal after the other, not speaking, but his eyes were bright each time when, by his efforts, a ram was persuaded to stand upright. Behind him, from the yellow water, each croak of a frog encouraged him.

But though he had never seen such teeming water-life before, he wouldn't let himself do more than glance in its direction. If he was still at Gulla Tank tomorrow, perhaps Mr. Tucker would let him walk out here—or even ride Bender—to observe these wonders. In the meantime these rams had to be saved.

They were working on the last half dozen just as Mr. Tucker arrived on foot.

"Good work, boys! I didn't expect to see half of them out yet!"

And, to Reg's embarrassment, he stood by and watched as they completed their task.

When all the sheep were on their feet, he helped move them up the slope to where green shoots were already thick, and they began to feed.

"They'll be right now," Mr. Tucker said. "I think we can move them the couple of miles to the other side of the fence. Otherwise the silly things will be bogged again as soon as we turn our backs. Jeff . . . I can see I can leave them to you two boys, and Bender and Punch, to bring along quietly. Take all day, if necessary. I'll drive the rest of the mob, myself."

Reg watched him stride off and mount his bike, Dixie

happy now to be on her own feet, rounding up the mob. They were a tough, long-legged mob, well able to travel at three miles an hour. With Dixie keeping the flanks trim, the bike beetled behind, weaving back and forth in a continuous figure eight, sometimes stopping and letting the animals get ahead a bit.

Bender and Punch started off gently. Punch knew that this small mob of twenty was still miserable and depressed, still ready to put its feet into the first boggy patch and stay there. So she took them quietly while Bender mooched along like a veteran stock horse, and the two boys on his back loved him and the rams with their heavy wet fleeces and their curly horns and the music of the frogs behind them that grew gradually softer.

And it was exciting when Punch shot away for a moment or two, and brought back a "straggler" ewe she had glimpsed through the mulga scrub. Its fleece was hanging almost to the ground, torn, untidy, and dirty.

"She's missed the last couple of musters," Jeff estimated. "Carrying at least two seasons' wool."

Reg said, "I'd like to know all about sheep, like you do."

"It's very easy," said Jeff, who had been imbibing sheep knowledge since the day he was born. "Just sort of comes to you."

Reg felt encouraged. If Jeff said it wasn't too difficult to learn, then it couldn't be. He had already recognized that Jeff was a bloke whose word was never uttered lightly; later on, no doubt, when he was old, he'd be rather like his old man.

They drove those sheep quietly, letting them nibble their way. It wasn't long before the mob ahead was out of sight, and the musterer and the throaty bike out of hearing.

As they jogged they talked a little, comfortably, about the

rain, the water-life that appeared so amazingly and seemingly from nowhere, about the feed that was coming up so rapidly. They never talked about Reg's problems.

In fact it was not until they were back in Gulla Tank kitchen that Reg realized he hadn't thought once about his troubles out there in the paddocks with Jeff.

## Chapter **Eighteen**

CHRIS WAS SURPRISED and pleased with Reg's interest and ability in the outdoor work. "That boy could do well in this country—if he waked up to himself," he told Mary one night, after the young people had gone to bed. "He has the same feel for it as Jeff, and a feel for the stock he handles."

"Yes, he could," Mary agreed, "but the way things are going with him, Chris, he'll never have the opportunity or the education to be anything better than a station handy-man."

"As I just said, Mary, he has to wake up to himself *first*."

And when Chris made a statement in that tone of voice, Mary always smiled and changed the subject.

During these days of waiting, Sylvie was exempt from the School-of-the-Air lessons. Mary knew that Sylvie had no mind for book learning at this moment. Neither did they discuss the future. They both knew that the future, now, was something which must unfold itself.

So Mary filled in the girl's time with sewing and cooking lessons. She produced one of her own cotton dresses—not the yellow with green flowers, but a pink that was still fresh and bright—and showed Sylvie how to alter it to fit herself. Mary was a good teacher and Sylvie soon found that she could not only hand-stitch hems, but also stitch straight seams on the machine. Before each mealtime came the cooking lesson—with Mary offering up thanks that the supply truck had come only the day before the rain started. On bread-making days, Sylvie was instructed how to knead the dough with the butt end of her fist as Mary did. But it was the sewing that the girl liked best.

And then as they were about to start breakfast on the fifth morning, with the sun brilliant in a cloudless sky, they received a phone call from the Homestead to say that the Land Rover had been able to leave at last. It would escort them into Kingoonya. And that, as there was a case already listed to be heard in the Kingoonya police station that morning, the two local justices of the peace, who had come in from outlying properties to preside, would remain in the town pending their arrival. Reg would be charged by the Kingoonya police officer with willful damage.

Mr. Tucker came from the phone with sober face.

"You probably don't know much about these court matters, Reg," he said. "Do you realize you will have to plead either 'Guilty' or 'Not Guilty'?"

"Yes," Reg said, his eyes on the bowl of breakfast food in front of him. "I . . . I've been through it before, Mr. Tucker."

"Of course, I'd forgotten."

Mr. Tucker took up his position on the hearth, and picked up the cat whose tail had suffered as he took his stand. He soothed it absent-mindedly.

"What are you going to plead, Reg?"

"I . . . I guess I'm . . . guilty," said the boy.

There was silence in the kitchen except for the scrape of a spoon on a bowl as the Tucker boys tried to keep the atmosphere near normal by continuing with the routine of breakfast.

"I think you're wise, Reg," Mr. Tucker said at last. "I'll have a word with the officer in charge as soon as we arrive."

"Do you think they'll . . . take Reg away?" Sylvie said.

"I don't know, Sylvie. You told me yourself, didn't you, that Reg had received his last warning?"

"Yes."

"Then we can just wait . . . and see."

The Land Rover arrived an hour later. The driver was a jockey-sized young man in a checked shirt and a wide hat, with a stubbly chin, high-heeled riding boots, eyes wide with interest in the runaways, and a tongue quite unused to words. He lived usually in a little out-station hut, alone in the midst of the saltbush miles, with a small fox terrier for company. The fox terrier was with him now.

The whole Tucker family made ready for this journey into the railway town of Kingoonya—the "capital" of the South Australian northwest—and the point at which the Alice Springs-Darwin road swept north. An opportunity for community contact—no matter what the reason—could not be ignored. And with the Land Rover as escort, ready to give a pull out of a crab-hole, Chris felt confident in taking Herbie out onto the mulga flats.

They were a spruce group as they piled into Herbie. The Tucker boys were all wearing clean blue shirts, and Reg was no different from a Tucker boy. He and Peter were much the same size and Mary had given him a set of Peter's clothes, so that he looked as trim as Peter. He wore his own boots, still pinching, but polished until the toe tips were like black mirrors and rejuvenated with a set of new laces. Mary personally inspected his hair, his fingernails, and his neck, even though he squirmed.

Sylvie wore her new dress, a pair of Mary's stockings,

and one of Mary's petticoats. Mrs. Hedges' shoes were gleaming, too, and Mary had rolled the girl's hair again so that the turned-up ends were firm and tidy on her shoulders. Brother and sister could have been part of Mary's own well-cared-for family.

But they were a very silent family as Herbie followed the Land Rover out onto the track. On either side the water had raced in a flood over every slight slope, leaving behind piled-up debris of leaves and twigs against the saltbush. It had almost obliterated the old wheel ruts. Only the depression in the surface, slight or deep, the width of a vehicle, and a complete knowledge of the way, kept them on the track. Sylvie realized that had the rain come a night earlier and washed out the track ahead of them, she and Reg might never have reached Gulla Tank or, indeed, anywhere.

Already the country looked different. There was no dust and the air was clean. Certainly the conquering sun would soon cake and crack the earth as it evaporated the moisture. But in the meantime, the stretch of red country to the horizon was smeared, as though with a careless paintbrush, with daubs of green where before only the wind-polished gibbers had burned the eyes. The mulga was disposed to flower after a good drink and here and there were patches dusted with a gold wattle-like bloom. The edges of the track were hemmed now with the varied colors of the blue bindy-eye, the emerald green of the earth-hugging annual saltbush, the yellow Billy buttons. Once, in the very center of the track, a spray of Sturt pea winked its bold black eyes above its red beard.

Sylvie noticed it all and thought how interesting it would be to talk about this rapid transformation with Mr. Scott; Mr. Scott, who was shadowy now and distant, far back with the heat and the dust and the scorching wind of a few days ago. She was no longer identifying that runaway journey with Mr. Scott. The reason why they were in this car now, with Mr. and Mrs. Tucker and the Tucker boys, was lost in the dread of not knowing what lay ahead at Kingoonya. . . . An hour or two would see them there.

She forgot the colored threads that edged the track, she forgot her new dress, the first experience of stockings, and the turn-up of her hair, in the agony of thinking about Kingoonya. She sat very still between Chris and Mary Tucker, and in the corner of the back seat Reg, too, was silent.

The town of Kingoonya was not new to them. They passed through it when they went up or down the line, or when they went to such events as the Kingoonya Races. The town consisted of fourteen fettlers' cottages, a school, a teacher's residence, hotel, store, hall, and police station. The buildings, forming a square, sat on earth that was flat, bare, and red. In the center of the square was a concrete cricket pitch. Vehicles either respected it and drove around it, or didn't respect it and drove over it. An incinerator fashioned from a forty-four-gallon drum stood in the open space, and those who wanted could burn their rubbish in it.

Vehicles approaching Kingoonya from any direction saw from a distance that the town was ringed with a shimmer of light from the glass of broken bottles. Above, large numbers of crows flew constantly over the rubbish dumps.

The driver of the Land Rover waved a temporary goodbye as they parted at the cricket pitch—he to continue on to the hotel at one corner of the square where he would wait to escort Herbie home again, and they to the weatherboard police station at the other.

There was nobody on the square except the garage owner

at the far end, working on a repair job that spilled out onto the square. His hammering on metal was very distinct. There were voices coming from inside the hotel, but, apart from the Land Rover nosing the hotel railing like a boat nosing a wharf, and an old lazy kelpie sniffing his way across from one of the fettlers' cottages, there was no other movement.

With a raucous exhaust cough, Herbie pulled up outside the cream-painted police station and dwelling. Two men came from the door marked Office. One was the senior constable, officer in charge of the station and district, the other was Joe Edwards.

Sylvie heard Chris give a grunt. "That's him—that's the Joe Edwards I knew!"

The words registered, but that was all. Sylvie was conscious only of her father, and she knew that Reg felt the same. Reg was walking close to her, just a shade in the rear, but so close that every now and again their arms touched. It was like a connecting current—this meeting with their father was shared, their fear was shared.

The senior constable was a big fellow, with broad shoulders and square, lined face. They were surprised to note that he was not in uniform. Beside him, Joe Edwards looked more hollow in the middle than ever, and his eyes were hidden behind the heavy overhanging brows. He was wearing his best clothes and a tie, but the coat swung loose and unbuttoned as he followed the policeman.

For a moment they stood and looked at each other— Sylvie and Reg and their father. Sylvie couldn't tell the depth of his anger because she couldn't see into his eyes, but his voice was quiet when he said, "So you're found . . . at last."

Sylvie said, "Is Mum with you?"

Just for a moment the man opened his eyes. "No. The new baby is expected much sooner than we realized—any time now. Your mother's in the Port Augusta hospital."

"Oh-h. . . . " Sylvie took one quick step toward him.

Joe Edwards said, "She's all right."

Sylvie looked back at Mary who came quickly to her side. "I wouldn't have left if I'd known it was so close," the girl said.

"Your father said she's all right, Sylvie," Mary reassured her.

Then Chris Tucker came forward with his hand outstretched toward Joe Edwards and reminded him that they had known each other in the army more than twenty years ago. So—with too many people present for them to say much to each other—the embarrassment of the meeting was over.

"The two presiding justices are in my office," the policeman said. "We had a case here earlier this morning. They stayed on, hoping you'd arrive in time to get this business over today."

Reg was still close behind Sylvie, and she felt him shiver.

Chris Tucker turned to the police officer. "I think the boy would like to make a statement," he said.

The big man looked at Reg. "Is that so?"

"Yes," Reg said, and Sylvie knew that her brother wasn't hoping any more.

Joe Edwards looked as though he were about to protest, but the policeman spoke first.

"You can come with Reg while I write it down," he told Joe. "Mr. and Mrs. Tucker and Sylvie—would you go into my office, please? The boys will have to wait outside. Only people directly concerned with the case may be present. We don't have an open court for a juvenile hearing. For the same reason, I am not in uniform."

So, while the Tucker boys took themselves over to their old friend, the garage proprietor, there to argue over bikes versus horses, Chris and Mary Tucker and Sylvie went into the office. And the senior constable took Reg and his father to some room at the back. Sylvie kept close to Mrs. Tucker.

There were three men in the office. One was middle-aged, one a little younger, and the third was Clive Scott.

Sylvie faltered when she saw Mr. Scott. It hadn't occurred to her that he would be at the police station and his presence made her even more miserable and embarrassed. He always seemed to see her under poor circumstances. Nevertheless, she did wonder if he noted any change in her, if he noted the new dress, the shoes, the stockings, the hair. But if he did, he gave no sign.

The police-station office was a medium-sized room. There was a filing cabinet, cupboards on the back wall, two desks —one for the presiding justices of the peace, and one for the prosecutor and clerk of courts, the latter two offices being combined in the person of the senior constable.

Even without the two wide-brimmed brown felt hats hanging on the door pegs, it was plain that the two men seated at the first desk were outdoor men. Their faces were a rich brown except for a white band just below the hair-line which those wide hats protected, and their eyes were crinkled around by strong sunlight. The older man was big and heavily built, with a paunch, sparse gray hair, and old-fashioned steel rims to his glasses. The other was smaller, dark-haired, and the restless movement of one foot suggested that he was not as experienced or assured in this role as the older man.

Sylvie knew that both were managers of large sheep-stations. She hadn't seen the younger one before, but she knew that the older one, Mr. Edgar Turnbull, had dealt with Reg on that last occasion, and she wondered if this would go against her brother.

Chris Tucker knew both men well and, like Mary, had also met the schoolteacher. While they waited, the older men began at once to discuss the rain. With joy they recounted washaways, fences down, bogged vehicles, and storage tanks running over. They would always talk about it. Only the opening sentence would change with time. It would become, "The year when we had that rain. . . . "

Clive Scott did not join much in the conversation. He sat very straight, arms folded across his blue shirt, solid knees pressing against the cotton denim of his pants. His face was unsmiling, but he looked very young and uncomfortable in this police-station office.

Then the senior constable, Joe Edwards, and Reg entered the room. There were several sheets of paper in the policeman's hand, and Reg's face was hot—he was near tears, Sylvie thought—while their father's face was grim and tight and dark. She wondered, with a sickening retreat of confidence, what had taken place in the back room.

There was a moment or two of informality while both justices spoke to the boy.

"Well, we meet again, Reg—but I'm sorry it's in this room," Edgar Turnbull said. "Didn't I give you a warning last time?" He leaned halfway across the table to stare at the boy through those steel-rimmed glasses.

"Yes-s, sir."

Then the policeman took his place at his own desk and, with due formality and attention to correct detail, pronounced the court in session. He looked around at the gathering. "You will each address the acting magistrates as 'Your Worship.' "

Then came the swearing-in, and the outside world, the rain, the washaways, the sheep, went from within these four walls. The two men who were to decide Reg's future settled down to hear the charges and consider their verdict.

"Reg Edwards, you are charged—along with another young fellow named Timms with whom this court dealt at the end of last week—with wilful damages to a government schoolroom, and breaking Mr. Clive Scott's record player, valued at one hundred forty dollars; and you Reg, alone, with breaking a school window and frame valued at fifty dollars."

"Not . . . not a window!" Sylvie denied quickly. "He didn't break a window!"

"I'm afraid he did, Sylvie," the policeman corrected and turned to her brother.

"Reg Edwards—do you plead Guilty or Not Guilty?"

"Guilty . . . sir," said Reg, in a low voice.

And Sylvie thought, rather drearily—did she really know her young brother?

"Reg has pleaded guilty to the charges," the policeman went on. "He has also confessed voluntarily to another offense—that of cutting a telephone line."

Sylvie's head gave a little jerk. So Reg had confessed to that, too! Her eyes leaped to the justices. She noted the quick deep frown on Edgar Turnbull's brow, and the sharp look that the younger man thrust at Reg. Everyone in that room knew what the telephone meant to the outback. This would surely put him into that training school! She felt trapped as though she herself were Reg.

"I'll read Reg's statement," the senior constable went on.

Sylvie's eyes came back to Mr. Tucker. He was sitting with folded arms and one knee crossed over the other. He appeared to be studying his brown shoe that was so very different from his usual elastic-sided boot. But Sylvie saw surprise on his face, and realized that Mr. Tucker had not expected Reg to mention the severed wire.

As the policeman finished the reading, he looked toward Chris Tucker. "You found that wire, Mr. Tucker—obviously cut with a sharp instrument—and mended it?"

"I did," said Mr. Tucker.

There was silence for a moment and then the older acting magistrate, Mr. Turnbull, took a lapel of his coat in each hand and slowly smoothed down the fine brown tweed. But he was unaware of the tweed. He liked boys, all boys. In his capacity as acting magistrate he asked, in his heart, for the wisdom of Solomon. And no one ever suspected that such a leather face could send up such a plea.

"We'll deal with the charges first," he said, "those of damaging the schoolroom and window, and breaking the record player. We'd like to hear your evidence on these matters, Mr. Scott. Would you please describe the state of the schoolroom?"

Mr. Scott gave his evidence quietly, in few words. He made no attempt to elaborate, and brother and sister knew that he could have added much damaging detail.

"What is the value of your record player, Mr. Scott?"

"One hundred and forty dollars."

Clive Scott spoke flatly. It was plain that he was deriving no satisfaction from this court hearing.

The acting magistrate looked toward Joe. "You know, Mr. Edwards, that you're liable for this damage?"

"Yes," Joe said through tight lips. "I'll pay."

Sylvie shivered. She had no way of telling what her father's reactions were at this moment.

"And now," Mr. Turnbull went on, eyes contemplating the large blotting pad in front of him on the table, "there are other matters. Firstly, there is the self-confessed offense of cutting the telephone line. In this matter, Reg, I must tell you, you have the right either to give evidence on oath and be subject to cross-examination, or, alternatively, to make an unsworn statement. I must also point out that an unsworn statement will not have the same value in determining our verdict as sworn evidence."

Reg's worried dark eyes passed over his father to Mr. Tucker. He looked to the latter to be advised what to do.

"Evidence on oath, Reg," Mr. Tucker advised quietly, while Joe Edwards folded his arms tightly across his chest and did not look at his son.

With the preliminaries attended to, Mr. Turnbull proceeded. "Cutting a telephone wire is a very serious offense."

"He confessed it, of his own accord!" Chris Tucker pointed out quickly.

"No interruptions, please," the constable said.

"Did you realize that such an act could endanger life?" Mr. Turnbull asked Reg.

"I . . . I didn't think of it . . . like that," the boy answered.

"We all know what isolation is in this country," the justice went on, digging holes now in the blotting paper with his pen. "We all know that the telephone is often our life-line." He looked up directly at Reg. "I'm perturbed by this act."

"As Mr. Tucker said, it is offset somewhat by his voluntary admission," the younger justice said.

"Oh, I'm not minimizing the importance of confession,"

said Mr. Turnbull, "but, as I say, I'm perturbed by what this act could have done. Life could have been lost."

It was an undeniable fact, and again the room was silent while Reg sat with flushed face, staring straight ahead.

"And then there's this matter of breaking into the school-room, Reg, to retrieve some opals that, according to your statement, you had hidden behind the skirting-board. Your statement doesn't say how you came by the opals. I think you had better tell us more about it. Where did you get them?"

Then Reg told the story, as he had told Mr. Tucker, of giving a swagman a drink, and being paid with the pieces of opal.

"Give me the opals," said Mr. Turnbull.

Reg took the dirty piece of rag from his pocket and passed the two pieces of gem-stone to the justice.

"M-m-m. They're worth a lot of money, Reg—possibly two hundred dollars. Did you know they were worth a lot of money?"

"No, not exactly. The bloke told me to save them up until I was older, and they'd be useful to me."

"He told you not to talk about this—not to mention that he'd given them to you?"

"Yes, sir."

"Didn't that make you suspicious?"

"I . . . I don't know."

"I think you do, Reg. Did it occur to you that this opal might have been stolen? That it was strange to find a man carrying his swag with opal to this amount in his pocket?"

"Maybe." Reg knew he had thought the man was on the run, and that was why he had listened for news of a robbery over the next few days. But there had been no such news for at least a fortnight.

"What did the man look like?"

"He was a little bent-up bloke—with eyes far back, as though they were looking out from holes in his head, and a thin face."

"That's the description of the man who stole four thousand dollars worth of opals from his mate at Coober Pedy!"

"I heard about that robbery," muttered Reg, "but that happened a fortnight after I met my swagman."

"The theft was not *discovered* until a fortnight after it happened," said Mr. Turnbull. "Your little swagman had a mate, Reg—who had to go to the hospital for a sudden emergency operation. He was brought down to Port Augusta. The sick man trusted that little mate—thought he would just carry on with their work until he returned. When he did return he found that the little mate—and the opals —had gone."

Reg sat there greatly discomfited. The story of another mate who had ratted! How he hated such a mate. And he had helped him! Given him a drink of water, when extremity of thirst might have caused him to be caught.

"If you had come forward with your story then, Reg, that man might have been apprehended," the justice said sternly. "Instead, he got clean away—probably hiding out in New Zealand by now. He had a whole fortnight to get away before the theft was known. You admit that you were suspicious of him—thought the opals might have been stolen—and yet you kept quiet. This almost makes you an accessory to the theft."

Joe Edwards stood up suddenly. "That's being a bit hard on the boy, isn't it, Your Worship?"

"Sit down, Edwards," said Mr. Turnbull coldly. "I don't think you're in a position to offer any criticism here." He looked at him with some meaning, and Joe Edwards' arms flopped to his side, and he sat down.

Sylvie looked from one to the other. So Mr. Turnbull knew what her father had done! Everyone knew what her father had done—except his family! It was part of the trap that she and Reg were in, that they didn't know their father's background.

She jumped up, nearly upsetting her chair in the sharp awkwardness of her movement.

"Everyone knows!" she cried. "But me, and Reg, and the rest of us kids. Everyone knows! Even the Timms family! Why can't we be told?"

She was shaking.

"What is it you don't know, Sylvie?" Mr. Turnbull said, his voice quiet now, his eyes appraising her, noting every detail of her appearance.

"What my father did! No one's ever told us—we only know he did *something*."

Her eyes blazed suddenly at Joe. "It could have been *anything* . . . even . . . even murder!"

"No! No!" Joe's head jerked up at the stark words.

Mr. Turnbull looked from one to the other. "You'd be wise to tell them, Joe," he counseled. "Young minds have lively imaginations."

"You know so much—you tell them!" Joe said tersely. He, too, was shaking with the shock of Sylvie's attack. He had never imagined that his children had any suspicions, or even thoughts, about his past. "Tell them," he said.

"You mean that?"

"I said so!—didn't I?"

Mr. Turnbull looked at Sylvie. "Your father served twelve months in jail . . . for theft."

Sylvie sat down. She looked away from her father . . . to the door, to the window, to the floor. A thief. . . . Well, she had always known it was something. Nothing was changed, except now this something had a name.

"I think, at this stage . . ." said Mr. Turnbull, suddenly busy with the papers in front of him, "that my colleague and I must confer. Before any decision regarding this boy can be taken, there are aspects of this case which must be considered fairly and objectively, with due regard to their serious nature. My colleague and I will retire for a consultation."

# Chapter **Nineteen**

IT SEEMED TO those waiting that the two acting magistrates were absent an intolerable time from the courtroom.

At first, attempts were made at conversation. Mary Tucker, who had moved her chair closer to Sylvie, made a remark or two, remote from the matter on hand. She mentioned that she would buy a "baker's loaf" from the store before they left for home. "It would be a change," she said. And she would get some elastic, too.

Chris tried to talk to Joe Edwards, but the latter, with his eyes withdrawn, was unresponsive; while Clive Scott, who had scarcely spoken except to give his evidence and answer the prosecutor's questions, seemed burdened with what was happening. The senior constable wrote busily on sheets of paper at his desk. Reg fidgeted on his chair, scraping the legs on the polished linoleum ever louder and louder, until the policeman looked up from his writing and frowned a warning.

Sylvie sat quite still . . . just waiting . . . yet wishing, now and again, that she could tell Mr. Scott not to be so worried. It was not his fault. And she was glad that Mary's chair was so close to hers.

Then the two men returned. The younger man led, with firm quiet tread, unconsciously indicating that, though less experienced, he had had his full say in the decision. He again left it to Mr. Turnbull to be spokesman. The latter was quick to come to the point.

He looked at Reg. "We find the police charges proved, and the defendant guilty. As he voluntarily confessed to the cutting of the telephone wire—an act obviously done under stress—and as we're not satisfied beyond reasonable doubt that he knew the opals to be stolen, we are not proceeding with these charges. The decision we have reached regarding the boy is, we believe, for his own good."

The magistrate turned to address Joe. "In the light of your record, Mr. Edwards, and the boy's wanton act in cutting the telephone wire, allied to his failure to come forward with information regarding this swagman he met—not even telling anyone he had the opals—we see a serious lack of moral training on your part. A lack that could almost be described as an encouragement to crime!" Mr. Turnbull took such a firm grip on the lapels of his tweed coat, pulling the collar so fiercely down on the nape of his neck, that he shot forward. "You're a failure as a parent, Joe Edwards!" he thundered. "For his own good, we have no alternative— no alternative, I say!— but to commit this boy to an institution!"

There was silence in the little room. Sylvie found it hard not to cry.

"Then there's this matter of running away," the justice went on more quietly, turning to Reg. "I realize *why* you ran away. Having been warned by the police—and me— you were afraid of the consequences of what you had done."

Reg suddenly felt that his clothes, as well as his boots, were pinching him. He wriggled on his chair, causing the loose joint to squeak again, and the policeman and the two justices and Mr. Tucker and his father looked at him darkly.

"In running away as you did," continued Mr. Turnbull,

"you caused a great deal of worry, inconvenience, and expense to a number of people. Police were detailed to search and watch trains and road transport, and a plane was sent out from Woomera. This, in effect, was a great public nuisance, a waste of public money! In consequence of all this, we have no hesitation in saying that a period in a training institution will have, we are sure, a salutary effect on you."

Reg gulped audibly.

The acting magistrate turned several sheets of paper face downward, signifying that he was done with them, and swiveled in his chair to look at Sylvie.

"Now, in regard to this girl. We don't know yet what sent her from home—as it appears she had little to do with the wantonness in the schoolroom, and she knew nothing of the opals. We can only take it, Mr. Edwards . . . " with a sidelong stab from those gray eyes behind the magnifying lens, "that here, again, is some fault in the parental situation."

Joe Edwards opened his eyes wide to look at the acting magistrate, and slumped again.

"I . . . I intended to go back," Sylvie said.

"You may have been partly influenced by wanting to protect your young brother," Mr. Turnbull went on, ignoring her remark, "but I can't accept that as the full reason. Now . . . you were as much involved in this public nuisance as Reg—especially as you are older, and should have realized what you were doing. For that reason, I think you should explain to us *why* you left home."

Sylvie looked at Mary Tucker. How could she explain to these men the thing that had been so difficult to explain even to Mary—especially with Mr. Scott present?

Mary realized her need. "Could I explain, as Sylvie explained it to me?" she asked the justice.

"Well, yes, if you think you know the reason." Mr. Turnbull was brusque.

"I do." Mary turned to talk to Clive Scott. "Sylvie was upset because—following the havoc wrought in the schoolroom—you said you would not return to the siding to teach next year. She told me that this is the first year she has really been interested in school work—that she has learned more this year than all the other years put together." Mrs. Tucker smiled at the young man whose face was slowly reddening. "Only a teacher who is dedicated—for want of a better term—can raise that kind of enthusiasm, Mr. Scott."

Mary looked back at the acting magistrate. "Sylvie was looking forward to another year of Mr. Scott's teaching, Mr. Turnbull. She was upset when she found that this was not to be."

"I said she must go to high school," Clive Scott put in, ill at ease, simultaneously encouraged by the fact that the girl had responded to his efforts, and aghast that for the same reason she had been prompted to leave home.

"Sylvie knew there was little chance of that," Mrs. Tucker said. "In any case, she realized she was already too far behind to make a success of it. Disappointment threw her off-balance. She didn't know what to do. She wanted to talk to somebody . . . me. . . . "

If this was an oversimplifying of the reasons that had driven Sylvie forth, they were valid and true, and Sylvie and Mary Tucker believed that this was enough for the acting magistrates and Clive Scott to know.

"Why couldn't she ask her own parents?" Mr. Turnbull looked directly at Joe Edwards. Then he added testily, "Don't bother to answer—I know."

He turned to Clive Scott. "I think you must be a very good teacher, young fellow," he said.

And while Mr. Scott was trying to control the ebb and flow of color to his face, Reg stood up with further grating of his chair, causing the policeman to look hurriedly at the linoleum. "He . . . he took us on excursions," he said defiantly, prepared to be told to sit down. "I liked them."

Mr. Scott turned to him with surprised, pleased eyes. "Thank you, Reg," he said.

"And now, to get back to Sylvie," said Mr. Turnbull. "You don't look irresponsible. Your clothes are neat, your hair well groomed. My colleague and I are most impressed with your general appearance."

It was Sylvie's turn to color and, at her side, Mary Tucker's dark eyes twinkled. Her last twinge of conscience about leaving Herbie's brake on was assuaged.

"We can only point out to you the foolishness of your actions, and hope never to see you in this office under such circumstances again. As for Reg, we'll arrange for him to be taken in by a suitable institution. In the meantime he must remain here at the police station. We don't want to look for him a second time."

Mr. Edgar Turnbull gathered up his papers, straightened the harassed collar and lapels of his coat, and stood up, followed by his colleague. Judgment had been pronounced, and there was nothing more to be said.

Joe Edwards had nothing to say, either, even to Reg, whose young shoulders were drooping, or to Sylvie who would not look at him.

The two justices left the room, knowing that the senior constable's wife would have a cup of tea waiting for them in the kitchen.

Mr. Tucker held out his hand to the boy, and Reg was glad of the firm pressure. "It wasn't easy to confess about the wire, Reg. You did the right thing."

Mary put her arm around his shoulders, and then had to wait for a moment until there was no quiver in her voice to reveal her distress, before she could say, "It mightn't be as bad as you expect. . . . "

One by one the elders went out, and Reg started to follow, but the senior constable said, "No, Reg."

"Not . . . not right away?" Reg's voice shook.

"Yes—from this minute," said the policeman.

"Sylv!" the boy called to her, frightened. She turned back, kissed him. She hadn't kissed him since he was a little boy, like Billie. He clung to her as Billie did, burying his hot face in her neck, wetting her skin with slow silent tears. "Sylv. . . ."

He was begging for her comfort, her understanding.

"It . . . mightn't be long, Reg, if you're good," she said. "Please . . . be good. . . ."

The policeman was standing by, looking out onto the red empty square. Until arrangements were made for the boy, he would have to place him under lock and key.

"Come along, Reg," he said.          •

Slowly Reg drew back from his sister and followed the policeman.

## Chapter **Twenty**

SYLVIE FOUND HER father, Mary and Chris Tucker, and Clive Scott standing on the red square outside the police station, waiting for her. There was another car pulled into the hotel railing now, and a customer getting petrol at the garage; otherwise the town was still empty.

"Sylvie," Mary said, "if your father is agreeable—would you like to come back to Gulla Tank with us for a few days? Until all this settles down?"

Sylvie stood silent, waiting for her father to speak.

"You said Mrs. Hedges was looking after the younger children while your wife is in hospital," Mary reminded Joe. "I know Mrs. Hedges—she will look after them well."

"I want to go, Dad," Sylvie said. "I hate the siding."

Joe Edwards nodded. He knew she did not mean the stony slopes, the black rails, or the square house. She meant the life that she had lived on the siding; she meant his drunkenness and his ill-temper when he was drunk; she meant the outgrown dress and the patched pants; she meant the apathy that had hidden the value of education until Mr. Scott had uncovered it for her; she meant the way her throat was hurting because of Reg; she meant the understanding she had found away from the siding.

He raised his head to give Mrs. Tucker a wry half-grin. "You have done a lot for my daughter, Mrs. Tucker," he said. "I can't refuse."

The group stood awkwardly in the empty square. Vapor rose around their feet as the hot sun, triumphant again, mercilessly withdrew the bounty of the rain.

Sylvie felt Clive Scott looking at her, and saw in his eyes now the surprise he felt at her changed appearance. "You seem to have grown since I saw you," he said. "Your frock suits you." There was a different tone to his voice. It was not teacher to pupil, but a young man to a girl.

"Thank you, Mr. Scott," Sylvie said, as a girl would reply to a young man. Her voice was steady and her face did not change color. But it was a moment of her life that she would remember forever. Not just because Mr. Scott had spoken so politely to her, or because he had paid her a compliment, but because both of these things made her a person. She was Sylvie. . . . Her head tilted a little.

Then Chris said, "How are you going to get back to the siding, Joe?"

"The Trans will be going through this evening—I'll go back on her."

"That's a long wait—I'll take you and Clive in the Land Rover now. Bluey can drive my family back to Gulla Tank in Herbie. We came here without bogging—no doubt they can go back the same way."

"There's no need," Joe said, but not very determinedly. He seemed uncertain of himself.

"I'd like to," Chris said.

And so it was arranged.

The evening meal was just over when Chris reached home, nearly three hours after Herbie. Mary was just beginning to wash up when they heard the Land Rover pull up. A big smile immediately creased Bluey's face. "Now I can get back to the Homestead," he said, using more words at once

than he had said all day. "They're having a film there tonight—boss brought it back from Adelaide. Don't want to
miss it."

Mary was relieved to see Bluey go. She had never known
a young man with less to say than Bluey. Even she couldn't
keep up a one-sided conversation.

Chris sent the boys to bed early, even Jeff who, from his
extra height, looked ready to protest. But Chris gave him a
slap on the back, and said, "Jeff—you look tired, you need
an extra hour's sleep."

Jeff took the hint and followed his younger brothers to
bed.

"I want to talk to you, Sylvie, about your father," Chris
said, when they had gone. "I want to talk to you tonight—
while this thing is raw in your mind—while you're hurt."

Sylvie looked toward him, wishing she didn't have to
listen, wondering if she was any more hurt now than before
she had run away, no longer wanting to hear the details of
what he had done.

"I had a long talk with your father after we reached the
siding—he seemed to want to talk. You see, I knew him
quite well during the war. As I told you, the Joe Edwards
I knew then was a likable sort—nothing polished about
him and a bit of a ragamuffin, but always ready to do a
mate a favor. And he was a good soldier. That's why I
was doubtful, I must admit, that the man I knew was your
father."

Sylvie looked up, interest developing.

"Your father was left an orphan when he was fifteen. He
took care of himself, doing laboring jobs, until he was seven-
teen when—in 1943—he bluffed his way into the army. He
was stationed at the Alice for a while—fought in New Gui-
nea—was wounded there helping a mate to safety. He didn't

get a medal—like many others who did similar deeds—but it was brave. I saw him do it."

"Reg would like to hear about that," Sylvie said.

"I'll tell him," Mr. Tucker promised. "Just at the end of the war, Joe met your mother. Her people were solid, respectable folk. Her father was a clerk in one of the petrol companies. They were secure and comfortable, even if they never had anything to spare. They didn't like Joe because he didn't have a trade of any kind, drank a bit, and had some doubtful gambling friends. They said he was a drifter. Your mother was very young. They managed to delay the marriage for nearly four years—until your mother was of age."

"Was this in Sydney?" Sylvie asked.

"Yes. To try to please your mother's parents, Joe did an army rehabilitation course in clerical work—probably because this was his father-in-law's occupation. He got a job in an office, but he wasn't really cut out for a close, indoor job. He grew restless, changed his job several times, not always to advantage—he and his young wife went through some difficult times. You were born a couple of years or more after they were married. Then he got a job bookkeeping for a firm who had a chain of butchers' shops. It was the best job he had had. Joe had access to and responsibility for the safe, where all the change and all the loose cash for the whole chain of shops was deposited overnight. There was always a fairly large amount in that safe. Then came the day when one of his bookmaker friends— who knew the set-up and of whom he was particularly fond— came to him and asked for a loan of three hundred dollars, just to tide him over for a few days. Joe had been six months in the job by this time, and while he tallied up the money every day, the management only checked and counted it each week. That checking had just been done. Joe trusted his friend and could see no real risk in letting him have the three hundred dollars for a few days. It would never be missed before it would be returned. He didn't tell your mother that he was taking the money from the safe."

Chris sighed. "The point is, Sylvie—the money was not his to lend. He had to steal the money in order to lend it. And that night—after he'd withdrawn the money in the afternoon—the management decided to have an unexpected accounting."

Sylvie made no comment. She saw Chris's point—a theft was a theft.

"In his first surprise and panic—and to give his friend time to produce the money—your father denied all knowledge of the theft. The management brought in the police. Joe admitted then to taking the money. He appealed to his friend to come forward and bear out the story of why he had taken it. But his friend had good reason to fear the police. He didn't come forward. Joe was convicted, and served a year in prison. It would have been longer, but his war record was excellent and he had never been in this kind of trouble before."

Sylvie sat on, silent. She hardly knew whether the story was better or worse than expected. But she did know that the effect was the same.

"He found it hard to get a job when he came out. Your grandparents were very bitter toward him but, for their daughter's sake, were still willing to share their limited resources. But Joe was bitter himself by then and would take no help from anyone. He drifted from one unskilled job to another. Your mother's people wanted her to leave him and go back to them. You were not very old at the time, but she stuck to Joe."

Just for a moment Sylvie's mind tried to envisage what the sequel would have been if her mother had not stuck to him. But then, of course, there wouldn't have been Reg and Ruby and Ann and Billie—and that was impossible to imagine.

"The worst thing for Joe was finding how hard it was to leave the past behind, especially when asking for jobs," Chris said. "Finally, he vowed he would get out of Sydney and never go back. He remembered this far-away outback country. He came out here and got a job on the line. Soon he was drinking too much. Your mother wanted him to return to Sydney."

"I know," Sylvie said. "They used to row about it." She remembered how frightening those rows were, how Billie would come and cling around her legs, Ann would take teddy and hide under her bed, and Reg would rush out the back door and over to Timms' house. Reg . . . whom they had left back in the Kingoonya police station. "Was he upset about Reg?" she asked suddenly.

"Yes—very."

"So he ought to be," said the girl, lips tight. "Like Mr. Turnbull said—he never taught Reg the proper things."

# Chapter **Twenty-One**

IT WAS OVER a week later that Joe Edwards came to Gulla Tank. Henry Hedges, the head ganger, brought him in his old Holden. It was a Thursday afternoon and Chris and the boys were out in the paddocks; only Sylvie and Mrs. Tucker and the cats were in the kitchen. When Joe knocked on the door the cats scattered to their various watching posts on top of the dresser and the mantelpiece. Their green eyes were very wary when the two men entered the kitchen.

Sylvie was wary, too. She eyed her father, noting that he was wearing his best clothes, was cleanly shaven and sober. She was disappointed at his arrival; she had hoped that she would be left a long time with the Tuckers. She was self-conscious, too, because she was wearing the clean cotton dress that had once been Mrs. Tucker's, her hair was combed, the ends still turning up, and there were sandals on her feet. She wondered if her father would notice the difference.

She stood quietly at the table, rolling the pastry as Mrs. Tucker had shown her, waiting to be told why they were there. She had to grasp the roller tightly so that her hands would not tremble.

Joe and the ganger sat awkwardly on the kitchen chairs, and then Joe said, "I've got news for Sylvie."

"Go into the sitting room," Mrs. Tucker said. "Not as hot

in there—away from this stove. Show your father where the sitting room is, Sylvie."

The girl led the way obediently. The sitting room blinds were drawn to keep the heat out, and she had to switch on the light. When she sat down in her chair by the fireplace, it seemed that the room sat down and waited to listen, too.

Joe Edwards didn't sit down. He stood there on the green rug in front of her, looking at her directly with those very blue eyes.

"It's your mother," he said. "We've got a new baby . . . a boy."

Sylvie looked up at him. "Is it . . . a nice baby?"

"Yes, it's a nice baby. Looks like Billie over again. But your mother . . . she has to have a long holiday. She . . . mightn't be home for some months, Sylvie."

"Oh-h."

"The years at the siding have done their job. I . . . I didn't realize what was happening to her—what I was doing to her. You know what happened years ago, don't you?— Chris Tucker said he would tell you."

"Yes."

"Well, when I was free—my only thought was to get right away. But I should never have brought your mother to the siding. We only had you then. She came from a good home. I ruined her. Later, when things were getting bad with us—she could have gone back to her people—and taken you."

Sylvie thought about that. So she might have been brought up in a place like Sydney, in a good home.

"She stayed with me," Joe went on. "I knew she was foolish—and that I was wrong—but I wanted her to stay. We just . . . scratched along . . . at the siding. Now, the doctor says she must have a change—before it's too late.

I've been in touch with her family, Sylvie; she's going back to them, until she's strong.

"What about the baby?"

"Your mother will take the baby with her."

It was strange to be together in this comfortable room, talking this way, talking of the past and the future. Never before had they discussed either. In fact, Sylvie couldn't recall a time when they had discussed anything before. Neither had Sylvie ever been so aware of the woman who was her mother, of the young woman who was so pretty in the picture, of the older woman who was so tired and not pretty any more. She wished, fiercely, that during all those past years her mother hadn't had to live at the siding—that there had been something in her life that would have kept the prettiness, kept her strong.

She cried quietly. She wanted to run into the kitchen and seek Mrs. Tucker's arms—who would understand why she cried—but she sat on because her father still looked at her.

"Will you come home with me, Sylvie?" he said. "I need you. Someone has to look after Billie and Ann and Ruby. The Hedges are being moved farther up the line—to a one-bedroom house. In any case, we can't expect Mrs. Hedges to look after them indefinitely. Not that she minds." A half-smile deepened the grooves in his face. "She likes those kids."

Through her tears, Sylvie said, "I don't want to go back to the siding. I hate the siding."

"Turnbull came to see me, Sylv—it seems that he happened to run into the doctor down at the Port and they had a talk. He told me I can keep the little ones at home—if you'll agree to look after them. You seem to have made an impression on him. Otherwise, it means a Home."

Even through the blur she saw that he was looking at her with the barrier of his age down. He needed her. His whole future depended on her cooperation. She saw that he was lonely and afraid, that whatever had been bad in the last years was as nothing to this breaking up of the family.

"You could manage, couldn't you?"

He was appealing now to her capability, attributing to her enough maturity. She supposed she was old enough. After all, she was more than old enough to go to high school. Mr. Scott had told her that she should have been there a year or more ago. Well, she had come to Mrs. Tucker to be told about the future—and the future had come to her.

She liked her father when he was sober, and today he looked so clean. But she remembered that he had once been convicted of theft—that that was why he had chosen to live on the siding. It was this that had taken away her mother's prettiness.

She was not pressing an advantage, but just stating a fact, when she said again, "I don't want to go back to the siding."

"All right, we'll leave," said the man desperately. "I'll get another job—I'll leave the line. I'll get something in the Port or Whyalla—how will that do?"

"D'ye mean it?" Sylvie said. She stared straight into the blue eyes—trying to see the truth in them. And around them she saw the crinkly lines that must have been made by laughter. As a boy he must have laughed a lot, like Reg, who—despite everything—still did.

"I promise, Sylvie—we have to keep together."

"What about Reg?"

Joe Edwards had been waiting and hoping for this question. "The boy's been fretting. Did Chris Tucker tell you?"

"No. I didn't know he'd heard how Reg was getting on."

"Perhaps he didn't want to upset you. Anyway, Chris knows Edgar Turnbull as a friend. He had a talk with him —told him he was certain that there was nothing really wrong with the boy. He told him how good he is with animals—how he's got his boss to promise he'll take him on as a jackeroo if he does well at school. Sylvie . . . he's to be given another chance—if you come home."

Sylvie stood up and sniffed the tears away. This was reason enough to query no more. "All right," she said, "I'll do my best."

They looked at each other and, standing together, Sylvie was nearly as tall as her father. She didn't offer any friendly gesture, even to touch him, nor he her. Perhaps he would have been glad of her touch, but Sylvie was not forgetting that such a short time ago he had struck her.

"The kids are out waiting in the car. I wanted to ask you before they came in. I wanted to know . . . if you were willing."

Suddenly she realized that he was asking her help in keeping the family together, when he could have simply ordered her home. She held out her hand then, for just one brief moment. And his touch was warm and grateful and strong.

"Ruby's upset about Mum not coming home for a long time," he said. "She was all right with Mrs. Hedges—but she kept asking when her mother was coming. I don't think Ann and Billie realize the situation."

And Sylvie thought—do I realize it?—do I understand what is happening?—that now they are in my care? She followed her father out into the sunshine, glad that, at this first meeting, she was wearing a clean cotton dress whose waist was in the right place, that her hair was shiny and combed, that there were sandals on her feet.

As soon as Ann and Billie saw her, they scrambled out of the car. Ann, being bigger, was out the door first and, in his disappointment, Billie reached ahead and pinched her bottom. Ann rubbed the spot hard but was too eager to reach Sylvie to stay and hit back.

They crowded around her, hugging her, and Ruby, being taller, put her arms around her neck. Sylvie could feel this younger sister's shaking.

"D'ye think she'll forget us—if she's gone a long time, Sylv?" she said hotly in her ear. "I don't want her to forget us." The big brown eyes were worried.

"Course she won't!" Sylvie said. "She likes us, doesn't she?—she's our mother."

Ann was the first to talk of the new situation. "Dad says we have to do as you say from now on. Help you with the dishes and make our own beds."

Sylvie looked at her father over the heads of the young ones. She knew he hadn't been as sure of her as Ann made it sound. And she was glad.